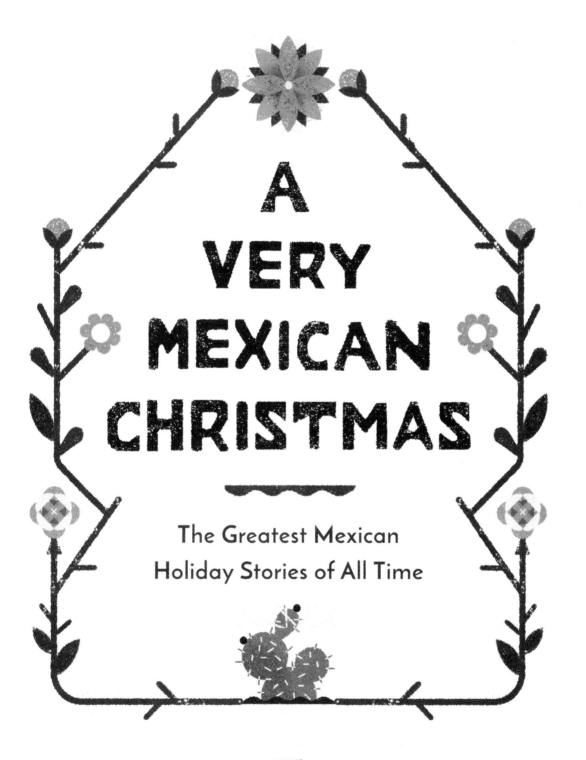

A VERY MEXICAN CHRISTMAS

The Greatest Mexican
Holiday Stories of All Time

NEW VESSEL PRESS

NEW YORK

 New Vessel Press

www.newvesselpress.com

Library of Congress Cataloging-in-Publication Data
Various
A Very Mexican Christmas: The Greatest Mexican Holiday Stories of All Time / various authors.
p. cm.
ISBN 978-1-954404-08-3
Library of Congress Control Number 2022931402
Mexico—Fiction

TABLE OF CONTENTS

A
VERY
MEXICAN
CHRISTMAS

THE TOPPLED TREE

Fabio Morábito

He heard Alfonso's mother walking in the upstairs bedroom and remembered that neither he nor Rubén nor Alejandro had ever gone up to the second floor, even though they had been frequent guests at the house for such a long time. There was still time to get away, he thought. Although he had mentally prepared himself to be greeted by a woman of a certain age, he hadn't pictured such a wreck and wondered if, when she answered the door and saw how much he too had changed, she had felt equally disconcerted. Maybe if he made his escape right away, she would be the first to feel grateful. When he told her on the phone, in response to her invitation to show his face one of these afternoons, that he could visit the following Tuesday, when he'd be going to a medical lab only two blocks from her house, her lilting tone had fallen slightly, as if she hadn't expected her invitation to be taken seriously.

He listened to the footsteps on the second floor and saw, on top of the piano, the cookies he had brought. In her hurry to go upstairs and find photos of Alfonso, his old friend's mother had accepted the cookies without even thanking him. Then he looked at the door and realized he wouldn't have the courage to dash out.

He would stay for half an hour and then would take his leave, inventing some commitment. He heard her come downstairs, and when she reappeared in the living room and told him she hadn't found the photos of Alfonso and his family, he was secretly glad, as he had no desire to review the predictable gallery of his friend's kids' birthday parties and other childhood celebrations.

"You shouldn't have gone to the trouble," she said, taking the package of cookies from the piano and depositing them on the coffee table. "Can I get you some coffee?"

He declined. Excused from that task, Alfonso's mother sank heavily into the armchair, and it was in that moment that they really looked at each other.

"How amazing, Antonio, you haven't changed at all!" she said.

"I wish that were true."

"I really mean it. Me, on the other hand, well, look at me—I'm an old woman. I climb two steps and I run out of breath."

"You look very well to me."

"Nonsense! When my husband passed away, I aged ten years."

She spoke to him in greater detail of her husband's illness, which she had mentioned briefly on the phone, and then she brought him up to date on the lives of each one of her children, concluding in a querulous tone:

"Ignacio's the only one I see regularly. He comes over for a moment every night to see what I need. It's on his way back from the hospital."

He vaguely remembered Ignacio, the oldest of the five siblings, stiff and incapable of producing a smile. It didn't surprise him that Ignacio was a doctor.

"You really don't want coffee?"

"Well, if it's no trouble . . ." And on seeing the effort it took for her to get up, he regretted saying yes and asked if she needed help, but his friend's mother said it wasn't necessary and she'd just be a few minutes. He waited there by himself, and his eyes were drawn to the Christmas pine that stood, still undecorated, in the corner of the dining room. On the floor were several small cardboard boxes that must have contained colored ornaments, and he recalled the afternoon when, with his typical clumsiness, he had knocked down the huge tree that stood in that same corner, loaded with lights and decorations. Half of the glass globes had broken. A few months earlier, while playing volleyball at the club, he'd had a dramatic fall over Alfonso, breaking his friend's arm. And a week or two after that, with Alfonso still in a cast, he had a face-off with his friend's father over the electric guitar that Rómulo, one of Alfonso's brothers, had lent him. The man dragged his two sons over to their house on a Sunday afternoon to demand the return of the guitar, which Antonio didn't have at the moment. He promised to return it the next day without fail, and so he did, but after that, whenever he went to Alfonso's house, he and his friend's dad had avoided each other. And that was followed two months later by the tree incident. It was an extravagant fall. His friend's father was upstairs, and when he heard the commotion, he came running down the staircase, but stopped when he understood that once again Antonio was the culprit, and went right back upstairs without uttering a word. Antonio offered to pay for the damage, but Alfonso refused. Even today, thinking about the series of calamities he had caused in this house, he felt a wave of shame and wondered if he hadn't come out of some obscure need to repair his ruined image, which his friend's father had carried off with him to the afterlife.

She emerged from the kitchen carrying a tray with two cups of coffee.

"You haven't unwrapped the cookies?" she asked.

"No, I was remembering the time I knocked down the Christmas tree."

"You knocked it down? Wasn't it Alejandro?"

"No, it was me," he said, disappointed that she didn't remember clearly. "I broke all the bulbs and colored lights."

"Did you say sugar or no sugar?"

"No sugar." He drew closer to take the cup of coffee. "You husband must've hated me. Before that I had broken Alfonso's arm."

"You!" she exclaimed.

"At the club, playing volleyball. He was in a cast for a month-and-a-half."

"My God, what a memory I have. You know, I don't remember. Maybe it was because Alfonso was always breaking something. Every so often he would need a cast."

He was about to remind her of the incident with the guitar, but he figured she wouldn't remember that, either. They remained silent, which created an uncomfortable pause, and he, noticing the serenity of the street, remarked:

"How peaceful it is here!"

"Too peaceful. I wish there was a little more activity."

He looked at the piano against the left wall, and without hoping for much, he asked if she knew how to play.

"I've taken it up again recently to keep myself occupied," she replied. "Would you like to hear something?"

"I'd love to," he said, and when he saw her get up with difficulty from the chair to head toward the piano, he wanted to help her, but he didn't move for fear of offending her. He figured he would hear one of those popular tunes arranged for organ or piano, so he was surprised when, after lifting the cover and removing the strip of felt that covered the keys, she asked if he knew Gounod's "Ave Maria." He said he did, and, after listening in suspense to the first chords, he was relieved to see that she played not only quite accurately, but nimbly. He saw her stumble only once, when she had to turn the page, and he stood up to help with that task. He stood next to her, watching her closely, and stared at her chubby hands moving along the keyboard as the upper part of her body swayed gently. When the piece was over, he said, "You play very well," genuinely surprised at her ability.

"I'm terribly out of practice."

"Alfonso never told me you played the piano."

"Because he never saw me play. I gave it up when Ignacio was born. At first it was hard for me, but then I forgot about it. Five children is a lot."

"Play something else," he said.

"You play too, Antonio; I remember very well." She stood in order to riffle through the papers piled on top of the piano and said, "I have something for four hands."

She took out a sepia-colored score, placed it on the stand, and told him to sit beside her. He hesitated for a moment before obeying. It was a short piece by Fauré called "Dolly's Garden."

"Do you know it?" she asked.

"No."

For some fifteen minutes they fumbled through the music, familiarizing themselves with the piece. They went back to the beginning to play it four-handed, but they got off to a bad start, their rhythms mismatched, and had to begin again. Then, as they went along, their synchrony improved, and they were able to reconstruct the piece from beginning to end.

"You play with great sensitivity, Antonio," she said, never taking her eyes off the score.

"I was just following you."

"We ought to play it all the way through, don't you think?"

"Yes." And he realized that her eyes were damp. He felt the contact of her arm. She gave the signal once more, and they started over. Now their synchrony was more confident, and though he hadn't touched the piano in a year, he was quickly transported by that frothy, agile song, whose melody seemed to want to drift away from a somber, opaque point, from a kind of limping cadence or warning that emerged regularly from the bass section of the keyboard and weighed down the joy of the high notes. And even though that ballast was the support that kept the most effusive part from losing its way, its presence was still agonizing, like a tuber struggling to push up through the ground. He imagined that this woman's life had been like that, a longing to fly that her husband's realistic low notes had muffled before extinguishing them altogether. He also felt some part of his own wavering life, always in flight but never truly adventurous, reflected in that music, and that his constant need to return and collect the remains of what he had scattered along the way, like now, finding himself ridiculously in the house of a friend from his youth, had prevented him from truly winging away and unfurling his abilities, keeping him fastened to a perpetual wound. It took him a few moments to realize that the other half of the piano had fallen silent. He saw that she was crying, and he stopped playing. His friend's mother covered her face with one hand, fighting her tears, while her other hand rested on the keys. He sat there watching her, not knowing what to do. At last he placed one hand on hers, producing a dissonant chord from the piano. She withdrew it and said, "The coffee must be cold; I'll reheat it," and she stood, picked up the two cups, and disappeared into the kitchen, leaving him alone again.

He got up and went back to the sofa, listening, but he couldn't hear any sobs. He opened the package of cookies that was on the coffee table, glanced toward the door, and wondered if he would be brave enough to leave at that moment. He imagined what Alfonso would say to Rubén and Alejandro: "They played a piece together on the piano; then my mother went into the kitchen, and when she came back to the living room, Antonio had already left," to which Alejandro and Rubén would reply: "He's always been a little crazy." He couldn't imagine any further conversation and concluded that having nothing else to say, they would change the subject. Or maybe she, with her bad memory, wouldn't even remember to tell Alfonso that he had come to see her, and that possibility left him paralyzed for a moment. Could she really be capable of forgetting his visit?

Because of course he had gone there so that his three old friends would know about it, not just to have coffee and cookies with an old woman. The temptation to run away was becoming irresistible, because suddenly he didn't care if Alfonso, Rubén, and Alejandro found out that he'd dropped by. Back in this house, which had changed so little, and among that furniture he remembered perfectly, he once more tasted the climate of mediocrity that had surrounded his friendship with them. Deep down, they had never taken him seriously. They were too normal to identify with his interests, and he, in turn, kept visiting them—though less and less often over time—because that normalcy attracted him, that way of receiving whatever life offered without making too many demands, because in a certain way they represented everything he didn't want to be, and that was the reason he couldn't stop seeing them.

She returned with the reheated coffee, and he noticed that there was still a trace of tears on her face.

"I'll have the coffee and go," he said. "You must have things to do."

"Me? Things to do? I wish."

"Your son will be here soon."

"Ignacio? He never gets here before eight, and besides, he'll be happy to see you."

"I'm sure here doesn't even remember me."

"Of course he remembers."

He thought that if he wanted to make sure Alfonso found out about his visit, he'd have to stay till Ignacio arrived. In truth, he had gone to that house to show his old friends, who had served as an inverted image of his aspirations, that he had loved them more than he had loved the people with whom he'd later had more in common. He glanced at his watch and saw that it was still two hours till eight o'clock. Another silence fell, and again his eyes returned to the pine tree in the dining room with the little boxes of colored globes beneath it.

"When are you going to decorate the tree?" he asked.

She didn't comprehend the question. Turning her head toward the dining room, she looked at the pine and understood.

"I should have done it already, but I get lazy. Every day I postpone it."

"Would you like me to help you?"

"Decorate the tree?"

"Yes." He calculated that the operation would take them over an hour, but on seeing her doubtful expression, he understood that the idea didn't please her, and he hastened to add, "Sorry, it was just a thought."

"There's nothing wrong with your helping me," she said.

"Maybe you'd rather have your grandchildren do it."

"I always do it by myself; no one helps me. I'd be glad if you gave me a hand."

"Consider it a way of making up for what I did that time I knocked over the tree," he said, and she looked at him as if wondering whether something more than a simple act of courtesy had brought her son's old friend to her home.

"This is your chance, then," she said, "but first, finish your coffee."

He said he would rather let it cool a little, and stood up and walked over to the tree. She also stood and explained something to him about the flickering lights, after which she kneeled on the floor and removed the globes from the little boxes.

"I'll have to buy spray snow," she said. "I used it up last year."

"The snow is the best part," he said, kneeling beside her. "It's the finishing touch."

They started attaching the globes to the little hooks to hang them. But then they realized that first they'd have to roll out the string of lights, so they had to take off the globes that had already been set in place.

"I always forget," she said. "First the lights and then the rest."

Once the lights were up, they saw that not all of them worked. Half the string wouldn't turn on. They tried a few times, swapped some bulbs. He said it was a problem with the cable and asked where he could find a hardware store nearby.

"There's one two blocks away, but it's not important. Please don't bother."

"I'll be back in five minutes. Meanwhile, you can finish attaching the hooks to the ornaments."

She explained where the hardware store was, and when he found the shop, noticing that they sold boxes of Christmas lights, he changed his mind, and instead of asking them to fix the string of bulbs, he bought two boxes of fifty bulbs apiece. He also bought a box of gold-colored globes and two cans of spray snow. At the last minute, he threw in two strings of silvery tinsel and a box of bright blue ornaments. By the time he returned, she had made fresh coffee, because the reheated pot had grown cold again, and when she saw everything he had brought back from the hardware store, she was annoyed:

"You told me you were just going to have the string of lights fixed."

"Like I said, this is a chance to repay an old debt, and I'm not about to waste it."

"All right, but first have the coffee and some cookies."

He went to get his coffee cup and together they arranged the two strings of little bulbs around the tree, starting at the bottom, and when they plugged them in, they thought the result was spectacular.

"My little ones are going to love it," she exclaimed, captivated by the contrasting effect of the hundred lights. "I have five grandchildren; the oldest is eleven, and the smallest one is two-and-a-half."

"There's nothing like kids to bring joy to Christmas," he said.

"I haven't even asked you if you have children, Antonio."

"A boy, eleven."

"How wonderful, but you ought to have another one; just one is no good."

"Yes," he said evasively, walking over to the tree in order to separate two globes that were very close together. She realized she had touched a sore point and tried to undo her mistake:

"I'm old fashioned, and I think everyone should have lots of children. I know quite well that you young people only want a few, and you're right."

He remained silent, and a stranger coming across the scene might have concluded that his presence in that house was something routine, and that she, despite being the owner, had a position subordinate to his, since it was clear that he was in charge of the tree, as if the fact of having bought a few things at the hardware store gave him the right to arrange the display to his liking. She placed the two globes in her hand on the floor, went to get her cup of coffee, and took a sip in the midst of the silence that had invaded the room, perhaps sorry for having let her son's friend put his hands on her Christmas tree.

"We're probably getting divorced," he blurted out, repositioning one of the globes. "In fact, it's already been decided," and he leaned back to look at the tree, while she, raising the coffee cup to her mouth, froze mid-gesture, lowered the cup, and said:

"It's not going to be a merry Christmas."

"No, we're not even going to put up the tree."

"You should really put it up, for your son's sake." And she took a step forward to stand by his side, as the two of them stood there enraptured, contemplating the hundred twinkling lights. Then she kneeled, left her cup on the floor, and opened the two boxes of ornaments he had brought from the hardware store, putting a hook on each globe just as she had done with the previous ones, while he placed the other globes on the branches, beginning with those on the bottom.

"Your coffee's going to get cold again," she said without looking at him, and he went to pick up his cup, took a sip, kneeled beside her, and said:

"The biggest ones have to go on the bottom and the smallest ones on top; it'll look nicer."

"It's going to be lovely," she said, and she glanced at him hesitantly, perhaps wondering how it was possible that this old friend of her son's, a man she hadn't seen in twenty years and with whom she hadn't exchanged more than a few polite phrases before this afternoon, could now be kneeling on the floor of her house, helping her with the Christmas tree. She emerged from her momentary bewilderment and started to hang the smaller globes on the upper portion of the pine tree, which was the easiest part, and for half an hour, they hardly spoke, both of them absorbed in their work. Only occasionally did they walk away from the tree in order to take a look and change the position of some ornament. It had grown dark outside, and she turned on a floor lamp that illuminated the living room with a quiet light. They finished placing all the colored globes, and when all that was left to do was to apply the spray snow, he conceded the honor to her, but she refused, and after a brief struggle, she put the other aerosol can in his hand so that they'd both be able to do it. They were surprised at the almost physical camaraderie that had insinuated itself between them in just a few hours, and for several moments they regarded each other with a tremulous shyness, a sort of disorientation which, while not sensual, was perhaps the closest thing to desire she had experienced in a long time. Feigning concern so as to hide her reddened face, she said:

"What will Ignacio say when he walks in and sees this mess!"

"Let me straighten up," he said, bending to pick up the plastic bag from the hardware store, but she stopped him with a decisive gesture:

"No! Leave it! A little disorder never hurt anyone!"

He let go of the bag and looked at her.

"Everything is always in its proper place," she said gently, conscious of having raised her voice, "and I don't know why, since nobody ever comes here."

He heard the sound of a car parking outside, checked his watch, and saw that it was a few minutes before eight.

"It's not Ignacio," she said, noticing his gesture. "He parks his car at the corner and walks over."

"It's late; I really should go."

"We still need to add the snow," she said, and in her voice there was an imploring note that made him feel uncomfortable. Suddenly he felt like leaving. He didn't want to see Ignacio, and he didn't care if Alfonso, Rubén, and Alejandro found out he'd been there. He left the spray can on the coffee table and picked up his jacket from the sofa.

"You're leaving already?" she asked, unable to conceal her disappointment.

"Yes, it's late. I need to go."

To avoid looking at her as he put on his jacket, he glanced at the tree and was surprised at how well it had turned out. He thought it was the best Christmas tree he had seen in his life. There wasn't a single superfluous ornament, and it radiated a calm, imperturbable joy. He wanted to sit on the floor and gaze at it for hours, the way people stare at a fire, till he fell asleep.

"I think it's better not to add the snow," he said. "It doesn't need anything else."

She looked at the tree, holding the aerosol can in her hard, and he thought she looked a little pathetic.

"Will you tell Alfonso I was here?" he asked, and his friend's mother looked at him again.

"Of course. Why? Do you not want me to?"

He looked again at the tree. "I don't know if there's any point," he said.

"Why?"

It was easier for him to speak while looking at the tree, so he didn't turn to face her.

"It's very unlikely we'll see each other again, now that he doesn't live in Mexico City."

"But he'll be happy to hear about you, Antonio!"

"I'm satisfied with paying off that old debt."

"The one with the tree?"

"Yes, maybe that's the only reason I came. Look at it. Doesn't it look wonderful?"

"Yes, it's lovely," she admitted.

"I've never had one turn out so well. There's not a single globe in the wrong place. I think that anything I might say to Alfonso is expressed better with that tree. What's the point of your telling him I was here? It'll be a secret between you and me. Don't go thinking I'm crazy," he added, noticing her staring at him.

"No," she said. They heard footsteps outside, and a moment later the bell rang. They looked at each other, and she made a small, panicked gesture.

"It's Ignacio," she whispered.

"Aren't you going to let him in?" he asked.

"He's got the keys." And at that moment they heard the key turn in the lock. The door opened and a tall man in a suit, around forty-five years old, on seeing him there, paused in his attempt to open the door and stood there with his hand on the doorknob. He really did have a doctor's face.

"Hello, son," she said in an uncertain voice.

"Hi," replied Ignacio, motionless, taking in the disorder of the room with a single glance.

"Come here, let me introduce you to Gonzalo, Señora Llano's son. She's an old friend of mine from Portales. Do you remember Señora Llano?"

The other man didn't reply. He entered and closed the door behind him with a dubious expression, trying to recall his mother's friend.

"He brought me some cookies from his mother, who's sick," she went on, her voice nervous and reedy. "And he helped me set up the tree. Look, all that's left is to spray the snow."

Ignacio came closer, kissed his mother, and offered his hand to Antonio.

"Nice to meet you, Gonzalo."

"Same here."

"What's wrong with your mother?" he asked.

"It's just the flu," he said.

"We've all got the flu; it's the season."

"Would you like some coffee, son?"

"You know I don't drink coffee," Ignacio replied.

"Some tea, then Gonzalo brought some delicious cookies . . ." She went to get the cookies from the little table and offered them to her son.

"You know I don't eat anything between meals," Ignacio said with a gentle gesture of refusal, and he asked, "How did you feel today, Mom?"

"Just fine."

"You look tired and your eyes are swollen, like you've been crying."

"Crying? No, son, why?"

There was a brief silence during which the son looked at his mother, and he, looking at Ignacio, recognized the almost-forgotten features of Alfonso's father and some of Alfonso's, as well.

"We're going to check your blood pressure; I don't like how you look."

"But, son . . ."

"Excuse me, Gonzalo." Ignacio turned around, headed for the stairs, and began to climb them.

"Certainly," he said.

"Son!" she walked behind her son with the tray of cookies, but she didn't add anything else, because the effort of climbing the stairs left her breathless. When she disappeared from his sight, he heard their footsteps on the second floor. He walked over to the staircase and thought he heard Ignacio scolding her. He heard the words "piano" and "Dad." Suddenly they stopped arguing and there was the sound of sobs. Then he hurried back to stand next to the tree. He heard the man's footsteps coming down the stairs and was afraid she had revealed his identity, but the other man said:

"I'm sorry, Gonzalo, my mother doesn't feel very well."

"Did something happen?"

"It's hypertension. She's in bed now. I told her she has to rest."

"I understand. I was about to leave, anyway."

"It happens to her whenever she plays the piano. I think I'm going to forbid her from doing it. It reminds her too much of my father."

"I thought she played every day."

"No, just every once in a while. She played now because you came."

"I'm sorry," he said.

"I'll walk you out."

They reached the door, opened it, and crossed the few meters to the gate.

"I forgot something," said Ignacio, and went into the house again. When he reappeared, he was carrying the two aerosol cans of spray snow. "My mother says for you to take them for your tree, because she wants this one to stay as it is."

"Thanks," he said.

"Give my best to your mother, and I hope she feels better."

They shook hands, and after he had taken a few steps on the sidewalk, he heard the other man close the door. He stopped because a shadow or a half-detected presence made him turn back. He raised his eyes toward the illuminated window on the second floor and saw his friend's mother waving to him from behind the curtain, and he waved back, standing by the gate, showing her the two aerosol cans in his other hand so that she would understand that he too would set up his own Christmas tree, no matter what.

2000

BIRTH OF CHRIST, WITH COMMENT ON THE BEE

Sor Juana Inés de la Cruz

From the sweet-scented Rose
is born the lovely Bee,
to whom the bright dew gave
its essence and purity.

No sooner is he born
than in the same currency
what he received in pearls
in pearls he repays, readily.

If the Dawn weeps, that's nothing,
just its habit, being beautiful;
but that the Sun sheds tears,
don't we all find it incredible?

If it's to water the rose,
such tender care is forlorn,
for there's no need of dew
after the Bee is born;

being intact in purity
like a nun in a cloister:
one with no predecessor
who can have no successor.

Then what good is the weeping
that gently plies her with water?
One who can bear no more fruit
and is barren, what does it matter?

But oh! the Bee relies
for his life on her, the Rose:
his dependence is always
so intimate and close:

for by giving him the pure nectar
that her sweet scents deliver,
she gives him life, conceives him,
and feeds him too, thereafter.

Mother and son, in such actions,
sacred, marvelous, dutiful,
neither is left indebted
and both of them are grateful.

1689

CHRISTMAS IN THE MOUNTAINS

Ignacio Manuel Altamirano

I

THE SUN WAS SETTING; the mists were ascending from the heart of the valleys; they paused for a moment between the dark forests and the black ravines of the cordillera, like a giant flock of sheep; then rose quickly to the peaks; broke away, majestic, from the pointed crowns of the firs, and finally wrapped around the rock's haughty face, titanic guardians of the mountain that had defied, for millennia, the sky's storms and the earth's agitations.

The setting sun's final rays edged, in gold and purple, the enormous turbans formed by the mist, seeming to ignite the clouds gathered on the horizon. They glimmered weakly in the tranquil waters of the distant lake, trembling as they withdrew from the grasslands now invaded by shadow, and disappeared after illuminating, with their last caress, the dark summit of that swell of porphyry.

The last sounds of day announced the approach of silence. In the distance, in the valleys, on the slopes of the hills, by the riverbanks, herds of cows rested, still and silent; deer crossed like shadows between trees, in search of their hidden shelter; the birds had sung their afternoon hymns, and were resting in their beds of branches. Merry pine bonfires were lit in the brush, and winter's glacial wind began to agitate the leaves.

II

NIGHT DREW CLOSE, peaceful and beautiful: it was December 24, which is to say, soon Christmas Eve would cover our hemisphere with its sacred shadow and enliven the Christian people with its beloved joys. Among those who were born Christian and, as children, heard anew the poetic legend of Jesus's birth every year, who could help but feel, on such a night, the revival of their first years' most tender memories?

Woe is me! To think I found myself, on this solemn day, amid the silence of those majestic forests, in the presence still of that magnificent spectacle transpiring before my eyes and absorbing my senses; having been so taken just a short while earlier with nature's sublimity, I had no choice but to interrupt my sorrowful meditations, and, locking myself in religious recollection, call upon all the sweet, tender memories of my childhood years. They awoke joyfully like a swarm of buzzing bees and transported me to other times, other places; now to the heart of my humble and pious family, now to the center of populous cities, where love, friendship, and pleasure in exquisite concert had always made this blessed night a delight for my heart.

I remembered my town, my beloved town, whose joyful residents celebrated earnestly with dancing, singing, and modest Christmas Eve banquets. I seemed to see those poor houses adorned with their Nativities and enlivened by the joy of families. I remembered the small, brightly lit church, from the gate of which the precious manger at Bethlehem could be seen, raised curiously onto the high altar. I seemed to hear the harmonious pealing that resounded in the half-collapsed belfry, calling the faithful to midnight Mass, and I could still hear, my heart pounding, the sweet voice of my poor and virtuous father, urging my siblings and me to finish preparing ourselves so as to arrive on time to church; and I could still feel the hand of my good and saintly mother, taking mine to guide me to Mass. Then I seemed to arrive, entering through the crowds of people dashing about in the humble nave; move forward until I reached the priest's feet; and kneel down, admiring the beauty of the images, the front door glittering with frost, the cheerful countenances of the *shepherds*, the dazzling luxury of the *Three Kings*, and the altar's splendid illumination. Elated, I breathed in the fresh and enticing aroma of the pine branches interwoven with hay that covered the handrail of the chancel and hid the bottoms of the wax tapers. Later, I saw the priest appear, dressed in his embroidered alb, in his brocade chasuble, followed by acolytes dressed in red, with very white surplices. And then, the officiating priest's voice, which rose sonorous among the devoted murmurs in the concourse, as the first columns of incense wisped upward, that incense gathered from the beautiful trees of my native forests, and whose perfume summoned something like the perfume of my childhood; still ringing in my ears were the joyous popular sounds with which the harp, mandolin, and flute players greeted the birth of the Savior. The "Gloria in excelsis," which the Christian religion poetically indicates is to be sung by angels and children accompanied by joyous pealing bells, the sound of fireworks, and the clear voices of chorus boys, seemed to transport me in an enchanting illusion to the seat next to my mother, who was crying from excitement; my laughing siblings; and my father, whose sad and severe countenance seemed lit with religious piety.

III

AND AFTER THAT MOMENT in which I consecrated my soul absolutely to the cult of my childhood memories, I moved, via a slow and grueling transition, to Mexico City, the repository of my impressions as a young man.

That portrait was a diverse one. It was no longer of the family; I was among strangers; but strangers who were my friends, the beautiful young woman for whom I felt my enamored heart pound for the first time, the good and sweet family who sought with their affection to soften the absence of mine.

There were posadas with their innocent pleasures and their worldly, noisy devotions; Christmas dinners with their traditional delicacies and enticing sweets. In short, it was Mexico City, with its singing people bustling in the streets that evening, enthusiastically engaged in "running the rooster"; with its Plaza de Armas full of stalls selling candy; with its glittering front doors; with its French candy stores, whose gaslit windows opened onto a world of toys and lovely jams. It was the sumptuous palaces spilling light and harmony from their windows. It was a holiday that gave me vertigo.

IV

BUT AS I RETURNED from that enchanting world of memories to the reality surrounding me on all sides, a feeling of sadness took hold of me.

Ay! I had gone over in my mind those beautiful portraits of my childhood and youth, but all that was quickly departing, and those bygone times, having said their poetic farewell, made my current situation all the more bitter.

Where was I? What was I? Where was I going? And an anguished sigh was my answer to each of these questions I asked myself as I let go of the reins of my horse, which was continuing slowly on its path.

In that moment, I found myself lost in that ocean of solitary, savage mountains; I was an exile, a victim of political passions, and I was on the trail, perhaps, of death, which the participants in the civil war so easily decreed for their enemies.

That day, I was traveling down a narrow and uneven path flanked by enormous chasms and colossal forests whose shadow intercepted the already weak crepuscular light. I had been told I would finish my day's travel in a small town of poor hospitable highlanders who lived off the fruits of agriculture and enjoyed relative well-being, thanks to their distance from the big populous centers and the goodness of their patriarchal customs.

I had thought I was already near that very desired place, after a day of wearying travel: the path was becoming more passable, and seemed to gently descend into the depths of one of the mountain's ravines, which looked to be a cheerful valley, judging by the sites I was starting to make out, the brooks I was crossing, the shepherds' and cowherds' cabins at every turn along the way, and, finally, that singular shape all travelers know how to perceive even through the shadows of night.

Something told me that soon I would be sweetly bundled under the roof of a hospitable hut, warming my limbs stiff from mountain cold by a generous fire, honored by those coarse but simple and good people, to whose virtue I had long owed unforgettable services.

My servant, an old soldier accustomed to long marches and the irritations of solitude, had managed to distract himself during the day, now hunting as we moved, now singing, and more than once talking to himself, as if he had called up the ghosts of his colleagues in the regiment.

He had advanced some distance to explore the terrain ahead and, most of all, to leave me freely to my sorrowful reflections.

All of a sudden I saw him return at a gallop, bearing extraordinary news.

"What is it, González?" I asked him.

"Nothing, my captain, but that, having seen some people on horseback in front of us, I went up to see who they were and make a report, and found that it was the priest of the town to which we are traveling, and his servant boy, coming from a confession and on their way back to the town to celebrate Christmas Eve. When I told them my captain was coming in the rear guard, the good priest sent me to offer you lodging on his behalf, and halted to wait for us."

"You thanked him?"

"Of course, my captain, and I even told him that we well needed all his assistance, because we were tired and had gone the whole day without coming across a single ranch at which to eat and rest."

"What do you think? Does this priest seem like a good character?"

"He is Spanish, my captain, and I think he seems like quite a man."

"Spanish!" I said to myself. That did alarm me; I had never met any Spanish clergymen who were not Carlists. Well, if I did not stir any political disputes, I would avoid quarrels and spend an agreeable night. "Let us go, González, to meet the priest."

Having said this, I urged my horse into a gallop, and a minute later, we arrived to where the cleric and his boy were.

The former approached with exquisite refinement, and, taking off his straw hat, greeted me courteously.

"My good captain," he said. "At all times, it is my great pleasure to offer my humble hospitality to the pilgrims whom chance brings to these mountains; but on this night, I relish it doubly, because this is a sacred night for Christian hearts, and so duty must be fulfilled with enthusiasm: it is Christmas Eve, señor."

I thanked the good priest for his affection, and of course I accepted his flattering offer.

"I have a modest parish house," he added, "as it is the house of a village priest, in a very poor village. My parishioners live off of onerous and sometimes unfruitful work. They are farmers and raisers of livestock, and at times their harvests and their livestock are barely enough to sustain them. As such, maintaining their pastor is an unduly heavy task for them; and while I seek to lighten it as much as I can, they are unable to give me everything they would like to, though, for me, I have everything I need and then some. Nevertheless, I find it necessary to inform you of this, good captain, so that you will pardon the lack, even as it will not be so severe that I am unable to offer you a good fire, a soft bed, and supper, which tonight will be appetizing thanks to the holiday."

"I am a soldier, my good priest, and I will find anything you offer me very good, accustomed as I am to the elements and to hardship. You already know the nature of this difficult profession of arms, and so I will refrain from making the speech already delivered by Don Quixote in a style impossible to imitate."

The priest smiled at the mention of the immortal book that will always be dear to Spaniards and their descendants, and thus, with good will and good company, we continued on our way, exchanging pleasantries.

As our conversation became more intimate, I told him I would be pleased to know, if it would not inconvenience him to tell me, how he had come to Mexico, and why he, a Spaniard who seemed to have been carefully educated, had resigned himself to living amid all that solitude, working with such coarseness, only to have as his sole prize a situation that verged on destitution.

He answered that he would satisfy my curiosity with great pleasure, as there was nothing in his life to hide. And to the contrary, precisely to undo the unfavorable caution that hearing he was Spanish might have produced in my spirits, since he well knew our preoccupations in that regard, he would be happy, in these first moments of our acquaintance, to refer to some of the events of his life as we made our way to the little town, which by now was near.

V

"I CAME TO YOUR COUNTRY," he said, "very young, intending to do business, like many of my compatriots. I had an uncle in Mexico who was quite well-to-do, and he settled me in a clothing store; but, a few months after my arrival, he noted that the occupation was exceedingly loathsome to me, and I was more content to devote myself to reading, sacrificing even my hours of rest to this inclination. He asked one day whether I felt my calling was of a more scholarly nature. I responded that indeed, the pursuit of letters was more pleasing to me; that since I was small, I had dreamed of being a priest, and had I not had the misfortune in Spain of becoming orphaned, perhaps I would have managed to find the means to realize those wishes. I ought to tell you that I am from the province of Álava, one of the three Basque provinces, and my parents were honest laborers who died when I was very young, which was the reason an aunt to whose charge I was given hastened to send me to Mexico, where she knew the aforementioned uncle had collected, thanks to his work, a small fortune. This generous uncle listened judiciously to my statement, and hastened to find a place for me in accordance with my inclinations. I entered a school where, at his expense, I completed my first studies to my great benefit. Afterward, having in mind the lofty idea of a monastic life, which until then I had known of only through the self-serving praise of those who already partook of it and the poetic descriptions I saw in religious books, which were the ones I favored, I began to seriously consider which order I would choose for the consecration of my life to the apostolic duties, the cherished dream of my youth. And after a thorough examination, I decided to enter the religion of the Discalced Carmelites. I communicated my plan to my uncle, who assented and helped me take the necessary steps to arrange my acceptance to that order. A few months later, I was a friar, and after the required novitiate, I took the vows and was ordained a priest, taking the name Brother José de San Gregorio, a name that was held in high esteem, good captain, by all my prelates and brothers, in the years I remained in my order, which were few.

"I resided in various monasteries, and I recall with great enjoyment the lovely days of solitude I spent in the picturesque Desierto de Tenancingo, where the only thing that perturbed me was the bitter shame of seeing that I was losing, in the idleness of a life spent not working, the youthful vigor I had always wanted to consecrate to the work of propagating the faith.

"I understood then, as you might guess, what the true value of the religious orders in Mexico was. I understood, with sorrow, that gone were the beautiful days when the monastery was an academy for heroic missionaries who, risking their lives, embarked on journeys to remote regions in order to bring, with the Christian word, the light of civilization; when the friar was the industrious apostle who would travel to a distant mission in order to don the crown of evangelical victories, bringing Christianity to the savage peoples, or the crown of martyrdom, in keeping with the precepts of Jesus.

"I begged my superiors a number of times to allow me to consecrate myself to that holy endeavor, and just as many times, I received negative responses and even looks of bewilderment, for my enthusiastic propositions were seen as contrary to the rule of obedience. Tiring of futile pleas, and advised thus by my pious friends, I turned to Rome to request my exclaustration, and after some time, the pope granted my request in a brief, which it will be my pleasure to show you.

"Finally, I was going to realize the unwavering ideal of my youth; finally I was going to be a missionary and martyr for Christian civilization. But, ay! The pontifical brief arrived during a period in which, beset by an illness that prevented me from making long trips, all I could do was hope to defer my enterprise until a time when I had recuperated my health.

"This was three years ago. The doctors' opinion was that, after that length of time, I would be able to consecrate myself to distant missions without any immediate danger, and in the meantime, they advised me to devote myself to less wearying tasks, like the care of souls in a small town in a cold climate, in order to ward off the risk of dying.

"That is why my new secular prelate sent me to this village, where I have sought to work as much as has been possible for me, consoling myself for having yet to realize my projects, with the idea that in these mountains I am also a missionary, as, before I arrived, its inhabitants lived in conditions close to idolatry and barbarity. Here, I am the priest and schoolteacher, and doctor and municipal councilor. Though these poor people were dedicated to agriculture and livestock, they knew only the principles that an ignorant routine had transmitted to them, which were not enough to raise them from the destitution in which they had necessarily lived, because the soil, due to the climate, is unrewarding, and because their position as it is, far from the large markets, did not yield what they would have liked. I have given them new ideas, which they have put into practice to great effect, and little by little the town has emerged from its former afflictions. Their customs, which themselves were innocent, have improved; we have established schools, of which there were none before, for children and adults; the cultivation of some mechanical arts has been introduced; and I can assure you that, were it not for the war ravaging the whole region, and that will continue to threaten it for some time, if the heavens do not take pity on us, my humble village would come to enjoy a well-being that seemed impossible before.

"As for me, señor, I am happy, as much as a man can be, amid people who love me as a brother. I believe myself to be compensated for my poor labors with their affection, and I am conscious not to become burdensome for them, because I live off of my work, not as a priest, but as a grower and artisan. I have very few needs, and God provides for them with what my efforts produce. Nevertheless, I would be ungrateful not to recognize the favors my parishioners perform in alleviating my poverty with donations of seeds and other goods, even as I try to ensure the donations are not frequent or costly, so as not to be an encumbrance, which is precisely what I have wanted to avoid in doing away with the parochial perquisites that are generally collected."

"You mean to say, my good priest, that you do not receive money for baptisms, weddings, Masses, and burials?"

"No, señor, I receive nothing, as you will hear from the mouths of the residents themselves. I have my ideas, which certainly are not the general ones, but which I practice religiously . . . While I recognize that a priest who is consecrated to the care of souls must live off of something, I also conclude that he can live while demanding nothing, contenting himself with waiting for the generosity of the faithful to assist with his needs. I believe that Jesus Christ wanted it thus, and it is how he lived. Why, then, should his apostles not content themselves with imitating the Lord, taking joy from their ability to say that they are as rich as he?"

Upon hearing these words, I could not contain myself. And, halting my horse, taking off my hat, and not hiding the emotion that had arrived even as tears, I extended a hand to the good priest, and said:

"Give me your hand, señor; you are not a friar, but an apostle of Jesus. . . . You have made my heart swell; you have made me cry . . . Señor, I will tell you frankly, with all my coarseness of a Republican soldier, that since my youth I have detested friars and clergymen. I have warred against them. I am doing it now in favor of the Reform, because I believed them to be a pestilence; but if all of them were like you, señor, what senseless man would dare, I will not say to unsheathe his sword against you, but to keep himself from adoring you? Oh, señor! I am what the clergy call a heretic, a nonbeliever, a *sans-culotte*; but here I tell you, in the presence of God, that I respect the true Christian virtues. . . . Indeed, I revere the religion of Jesus Christ as you practice it, which is to say, as you showed it to be, and not as it is practiced everywhere. Blessed is this Christmas that gave me my life's greatest fortune, which is encountering a disciple of the sublime Missionary whose coming to the world we celebrate today! I had been filled with sorrow, remembering Christmases past from my childhood and youth, feeling unlucky to find myself alone in these mountains with my memories! What were the parties of my childhood worth, if they were pleasant only because of the traditional joys and the presence of family? What are the unholy rejoicings of the big city worth, if they do not leave the spirit with but a fleeting impression of satisfaction? What is all of this worth when compared to the immense fortune of finding Christian virtue, that which is good, holy, modest, practical, prolific with its benefits? My good priest, please allow me to dismount and embrace you, and declare that I love Christianity when I encounter it in a form as pure as it was in the first beautiful days of the Gospel."

The priest, too, got down from his poor nag, and embraced me, weeping and surprised by my outburst of sincerity. He could not speak for emotion, and could only murmur, holding me to his chest:

"But my good captain . . . I do not deserve . . . I believe I fulfill . . . it is only natural; I am nothing . . . what could I possibly be! Jesus Christ! God! The people!"

1871

THE DOUBLE CAT SYNDROME

Carmen Boullosa

My season in hell lasted from November 1970 to July of the following year. It felt so long, I thought for sure it would last the rest of my life, that my only ticket was to misfortune. I was thirteen and had just barely become a woman—back then girls took a long time to mature.

Nothing made sense, and when I say nothing, I mean nothing. For example: the neighbors had a cat I used to see from my bedroom window, basking in the sun and grooming himself next to the glass door to their garden. He was black and white, which is how he got his name, Cow. Cow had a temper—on our block we said he was our guardian cat because at the slightest provocation, he would attack dogs, children, women, street sweepers, or other cats. Starting that hellish November, I would see Cow where he always was, and a short distance away, behind the neighbors' glass front door, I would see another identical cat, taking a nap on the rug. When I could, I asked the neighbor—who was my age—"Hey, is the other cat Cow's son? Because they're identical."

She replied, "Come on, we don't have another cat, Cow wouldn't stand for it, you know that."

"But I've seen him, inside your house," I said, and in response she looked at me like I was crazy.

From my window, I continued seeing double: one sleeping cat, and one kitty grooming himself. Today I have no doubt that no one else saw the second cat, only me. But things went on like that. For me every cat had eight legs.

AS IF CHRISTMAS WASN'T bad enough, there was also the horrible double cat syndrome. I've had an aversion to Christmas Eve ever since, but next year I'm celebrating with a tree, ornaments, twinkle lights, boxes wrapped in brilliantly colorful paper, holiday turkey, and codfish. I will sing Christmas carols and even put out a nativity scene. All by myself, to celebrate my life as a single woman, the way God intended. I'm going to give myself many presents, especially shoes from France and Italy. Those are the best. I'm not going to invite anyone. I'm not going to let them ruin the party.

THE MOMENT OF CHRISTMAS EVE dinner arrived—December 24, 1970. We all had to sit at my mother's heavy round table, the one she had chosen knowing we could fit eight easily, ten comfortably, and fourteen squeezed in tight. It was a table for conversation, lingering over a meal, a place to enjoy our food and try to be happy. It had once been the best place in the house. Today we were eight at the table once more, the six children of my mother (unhappy) and the other two (happy), my father and his new wife, a pair of lovebirds. She was eighteen, almost the same age as my older sister. She couldn't have been more than a year or so older.

My mother was in the French cemetery, or in heaven, depending on who's telling the story. In my version, my mother was in the house, wandering here and there, not leaving even to go out to the garden. At night, when we were all sleeping, she appeared, dressed in pajamas and a flannel robe, three-dimensional once more. Her footsteps sounded in the hall. She visited us six children, moving from room to room, bed to bed. She wanted to tell us she loved us, but the words got stuck in her throat. She spoke as if she were choking, making noises and croaking. It was very sad. It was terrible to be dead, far from us even as she stood there, and on top of that, there was what my father had done so quickly—a year and a day after her funeral—because there was no doubt they had buried her, regardless of whether eternal life exists.

To Mama, it wouldn't have mattered that he had remarried. In fact, she'd asked for it from her deathbed (that was one thing she did have, poor thing). But why so soon, and to this woman, this mean little brat, so heartless and charmless, poor as a bedbug, ignorant, and ill-mannered, lacking the slightest interest in the children of "her" Manuel? Because even though Mama continued believing that Manuel, our father, was hers, she was wrong. Now he was possessed, like a crazy person. He had become someone totally different, he no longer belonged to anyone. He was afflicted by continual attacks of anger. He spoke differently; he abruptly stopped reading and playing chess. He joined a sports club and took dancing and tennis lessons. His habits changed entirely.

But I'm digressing from the Christmas of 1970. Those eight seats at the bitter table. Forgive me for calling it bitter, I know it's self-indulgent, but it's true. Three days before, our stepmother had her stroke of genius. She ran to Luz, the cook, also nanny to the youngest children, and to Felipa, the house-keeper. They had been working for us for eight years, had seen the birth of the three youngest children and were now the ones giving us what little maternal affection was left inside those four walls, even though in life Mama had drawn a line, making it clear that they were employees. She respected them, and it was mutual, but they weren't part of the family. Our stepmother started by cornering them, pestering them with nonsense, and I say nonsense because she was nonsensical—but to her credit, she had the devastating aim that is the privilege of the stupid.

Then, to expand her turf, she fired the laundress. (It did not come as a surprise. The third one in service was naturally disposable, because Luz and Felipa had made an everlasting alliance, and their disputes and complicity were kept between themselves.) She replaced her with someone sillier, uglier, younger, and of humbler origin. (Neither Luz nor Felipa met these requirements.) Her name was Laura. She was fat, so we nicknamed her the War Tank, for her belly, for her ugly attitude, and for her coloring, which was more green than anything else, like she had some mysterious illness. Then, once Laura had become devoted to her, she ran to Luz and Felipa just before Christmas to tell them they were fired. Stupid Laura immediately brought in her brother's girlfriend. I don't remember her name, another almost exactly like Laura, not as ugly but even stupider, who followed our stepmother around like a puppy.

TODAY, AT THE TABLE on Christmas Eve, what hurts us the most is that Luz and Felipa aren't here. The new women heed only my father's wife and her orders. The table has become our stepmother's territory. The three enemies covered it with the most bizarre things. Tablecloths of various sizes, colors, and patterns are piled haphazardly, one on top of the other. Mismatched plates add to the disorder, and food that anyone would have considered repugnant is plunked down unceremoniously.

"*Nopalitos* with what?" asks Julio, the oldest of the boys, going on eight years old. His question is innocent, he wants an answer about the vegetable. He's always looking on the bright side.

"And what's that other thing?" asks Male, the one who follows me around, with a critical tone precocious for her nine years. The food disgusts us all.

"Eat!" Papa gives the order with a spike of fury that passes quickly, because the lovebirds are happy. They give each other pecks between bites, and don't let go of each other's hands except to wipe their mouths with their napkins. What are they wiping away? The saliva from their kisses, or the salsas, which are so dark and disgusting? Because the food is definitely disgusting, slimy. I already tried it. Where is the cod and the Christmas Eve turkey? They're gone, just like Luz and Felipa.

Mónica, who isn't yet three, begins to cry. Julio jumps from his chair to comfort her and I make as if to follow him.

"Leave her alone!" says Papa, dropping his lovebird façade. "Sit down! Don't get up in the middle of dinner, especially on Christmas! Mónica, eat! And don't you dare have a tantrum, or I'll give you a hiding!"

"Hiding, what's that?" Mónica doesn't even know the word. I do, because I've heard it in school. Mother had never permitted it, she would've never even used the word, let alone actually do it. *"A hiding! What a notion!"* I think.

I won't bore you with the details of the dinner, which, on top of everything else, runs too long. Anytime one of the children wants to say something, Papa shushes us, now in a festive tone:

"You can't do two things at once," he repeats, as if he's not only a lovebird, but also a parakeet.

The Christmas tree our stepmother put up is artificial and white; its attempt to look snow-covered only makes it appear albino. Nothing like the enormous, fragrant pines Mama used to buy. At the foot of the tree there are only two gift boxes, one for each of the lovebirds. His for her, hers for him, with cards. We inspected them in the afternoon, before they called us to dinner, even though we weren't supposed to.

We go to bed as soon as we get up from the table, no carols or opening presents. The lovebirds don't open theirs, either. "They're for tomorrow," she says to him; he's impatient to see her open her little box. The little that we had for dinner rumbles in our stomachs, refusing to settle. It's as if the chewed, undigested food is grooming itself, just like the neighbor's cat, Cow, did. I feel spasms as the food seems to perform licking motions in my stomach.

The lovebirds try to lull us to sleep by making strange noises in their room. My older sister summons us to the little ones' room (she whispers: here we can't hear their lovemaking) and begins to sing her favorite carol: "But look how they quake, the fishes in the sea, look how they quake, to see God born." My other siblings sing with her. I can't. I've lost my voice. I think of my cousins, my grandmother—their stews, and above all their desserts, the twinkling lights and the piñatas and the presents of other Christmases, and the games my aunts and uncles organized for us. We never believed in Santa Claus. Our mother never told us lies—never. We would open the presents on Christmas Eve, with all my mother's family, because they were our family, too. But my father had put an end to it. "We have to be by ourselves, it's time for us to come closer together," I heard him say on the phone to my Uncle Oscar a couple weeks ago. I'm sure they hadn't pictured the Christmas Eve the lovers prepared for us, either. The truth is, I had expected a special surprise—fantastic presents, or a big shared gift—maybe a house at the beach, like the one we used to have, that Papa lost during a bad stretch at the factory?

AND SO AS MY SIBLINGS sing, I am struck by melancholy. Julio and Javier take the container of clay out of the jumbled toy box. Felipa had been the one to keep it in order. With Male, they set to making a nativity scene: "Look, the Virgin Mary," and "I'll make the little donkey." I put aside my regrets and worries when they start making the baby out of green clay.

"Not green!" I object. "It's going to look like it's Laura's baby."

"The War Tank's baby?" says Male, mockingly.

My comment makes my siblings laugh, chasing away my melancholy.

"Come on," says Javier, "this green is beautiful, like a green plant, not a tacky green."

Javier uses a white button for the face, which makes us laugh, and a thread makes dimples for its eyes and nose. We draw on a mouth with a red pen. The little Jesus has no arms, "but it doesn't matter, look, he's a tamale, like a newborn wrapped it in its blanket." We sing, "between an ox and a mule, God is born," and then we go to bed, our hands smelling of clay and black with dirt, without even brushing our teeth. I stay in the little ones' room. I want to sleep in Male's bed, so I offer her a little of my allowance so she'll let me, but she refuses. Mónica sees her opportunity and convinces me to sleep in her bed, she wants someone to hold her and help her get to sleep, to spend the whole night like that. Having to hold her keeps me awake, but since I'm scared of Mama's nighttime visit, I promise to hold her all night.

My fear embarrasses me. After all, it's my mother. I miss her. I want to see her. But I'm overwhelmed by my fear of death, even though I try to convince myself that it's better to see her this way than not at all. What would be better? For your mother to disappear without a peep, or for her to come back even though she can't speak? Now it's my mother who, when she comes at night, looks fake, like Santa Claus.

At four-thirty in the morning I was woken up by what sounded like the end of the world. Bright flashing lights broke through the darkness. The sky shone red, white, red, white. I heard one of the horses of the apocalypse screech sharply, then I heard another of the horsemen arrive, this one riding a cow, it seemed. Unlike the neighbors' cat, this was a totally black cow, enormous and real. It mooed. Shouts. Doors slamming. Fighting. Voices. I thought I heard the doorbell. They were coming for us, who? Who? Terrified, with my heart practically beating out of my chest, I squeezed my eyes shut. I was trembling with fear.

My little sister Mónica woke up.

"What's happening?"

This was too much. If it was just me who heard Mama, who was scared to death at night, that would be okay. But the others sharing my nighttime panic was intolerable. I summoned all my courage, telling myself that Mónica had caught my terror because I was trembling, so I told myself not to panic. I held her tight and put my hand over her eyes, covering her lids.

"There's nothing happening, little one. Go to sleep. *Shh, shh, shh.*"

I comforted her, singing about this and that, about Santa Ana, San José, and a child crying over a lost apple. Finally the apocalyptic scene passed. Total darkness returned and I could no longer hear the horsemen and their horses, or footsteps or shouts. I stopped grinding my teeth. Mónica fell asleep, and then I did, too. That night Mama didn't appear.

The next morning, no one made us breakfast. Papa wasn't there, and we when peeked into the garage, we didn't see his car. We opened a box of cornflakes and ate them by the handful until they were all gone. Our stepmother finally appeared, her face even uglier than usual. But soon she cheered up. A smile lit up her ugliness.

She explained, like it was the funniest thing in the world:

"Who saw her, so withered, walking away like a hooker?"

That was the first thing she said. I didn't understand what she meant by "withered," neither did my siblings, and Mónica asked first:

"Withered, how?"

Our stepmother ignored her question. She didn't even look at her. Instead she began to tell us the following story, gleefully, like it was the best joke she'd heard all year:

"Laura gave birth last night in the servant's bathroom! She wasn't fat after all, she was pregnant and wearing a girdle! The baby was born alive, and started crying. The crying woke up her sister-in-law, who burst into the bathroom and discovered Laura wrapping the umbilical cord around the newborn's neck and strangling him with it.

"What's an umbilical cord?" asked Mónica.

Our stepmother ignored her again.

"Laura's sister-in-law," our stepmother continued, "tried to stop it. She must have; her hands were covered in blood." Here my older brother took Male and Mónica's hands and said,

"We're getting out of here."

Our stepmother said:

"No one is going anywhere, I'm speaking, what disrespect! I'm going to tell your father!"

She continued: "With her hands covered in blood, her sister-in-law came to wake us up, and we called the police and the Red Cross.

"And your father," she said to finish, very satisfied, "isn't here because he went from the municipality directly to the office. There was a problem in the factory! Like always! He's inept!" She sighed. "He doesn't even know how to dance!"

MAMA ADORED "HER MANUEL," she could find no fault with him. I didn't know if she could hear our stepmother insulting our father in front of the little ones, but the attack on her beloved would've left her fuming.

But I didn't see any fumes. The daylight prevented any supernatural manifestations.

When our stepmother finished speaking, we went to the little ones' room. Later, as she had threatened, she'd complain to our father about our "vulgarity," she'd say we had left her talking to herself (false) and that we'd eaten all "her" cornflakes (true).

We desperately needed to ask questions, because there had been so many things we didn't understand. The worst part was that there was no one to explain things to us. About the umbilical cord, for example. In Catholic school, in biology class, we'd gotten halfhearted lessons on childbirth, basic like the rest of our education, since at the end of the day we were only girls, but either we hadn't paid enough attention to the cord or they'd left that out. My older sister said, like she knew:

"The important thing is that the baby was born."

"But she killed him!" explained Javier, who understood the situation, even though he was only five years old. My older sister was incapable of understanding such a horrible thing. "His mother strangled him, don't be stupid," Javier added, so there would be no doubt.

"Don't call me stupid."

"Sorry."

Male added, before we could leave behind the subject of the Christmas murder:

"It has to happen that way, or else how can he be born again the next year?"

The rest of that Christmas passed without incident. My grandmother came and dropped off some delicious cod cakes. Our stepmother didn't invite her in. She also brought us presents, which we opened standing up at the table—dresses, little suits, shirts, and lovely blouses, in boxes wrapped in colorful paper.

Other than eating the cakes, we didn't do anything that day, we didn't even try on the clothes. We felt like flies hitting against glass.

The garden next door was empty. Cow wasn't there, and I couldn't see his reflection sleeping behind the glass door.

Not only did the world not end on Christmas Eve, it continued with a day as long-lived as a mummy. Who knows how, but somehow that cursed December 25 finally ended.

In the middle of the night, I woke up in my bed, but it wasn't Mama's footsteps that jolted me out of sleep. Even though her visits scared me, I preferred her presence to the things I didn't understand. That feeling was worse than hearing my own death approaching, worse than hearing her growl, unable to form words; worse than knowing she was sad, betrayed, humiliated by the lovebirds. I got up from my bed, walking quickly toward the little ones' room to get away. All of them were asleep. But there was something else there, something that seemed to flutter, something I couldn't see, that began to brush against me, frozen.

Mónica's bedside lamp was on. Its light fell directly on the little clay Jesus that Javier had made. The button he'd added to the face was gone, and so was the upper part of its head. It was also missing the other end of its body, where the feet used to be. It looked like someone had bitten the figurine from top to bottom, leaving imprints that seemed to be tooth marks. "How disgusting," I thought, and I got into bed with Mónica, held her tight, and, after waiting for a long while, finally fell asleep.

2014

THE DISCOMFITING BROTHER

Carlos Fuentes

I

DON LUIS ALBARRÁN had his house in order. When his wife, Doña Matilde Cousiño, died, he was afraid that as a widower, his life would become disorganized. At the age of sixty-five, he felt more than enough drive to continue at the head of the construction company La Pirámide. What he feared was that the rear guard of that other security, Doña Matilde's domestic front, would collapse, affecting his life at home as well as his professional activities.

Now he realized there was nothing to fear. He transferred the same discipline he used in conducting his business to domestic arrangements. Doña Matilde had left a well-trained staff, and it was enough for Don Luis to repeat the orders of his deceased wife to have the household machinery continue to function like clockwork. Not only that: At first the replacement of the Señora by the Señor caused a healthy panic among the servants. Soon fear gave way to respect. But Don Luis not only made himself respected, he made himself loved. For example, he found out the birthday of all his employees and gave each one a gift and the day off.

The truth is that now Don Luis Albarrán did not know if he felt prouder of his efficiency in business or his efficiency at home. He gave thanks to Doña Matilde and her memory that a mansion in the Polanco district, built in the 1940s when neocolonial residences became fashionable in Mexico City, had preserved not only its semi-Baroque style but also the harmony of a punctual, chronometric domesticity in which everything was in its place and everything was done at the correct time. From the garden to the kitchen, from the garage to the bathroom, from the dining room to the bedroom, when he returned from the office, Don Luis found everything just as he had left it when he went to work.

The cook, María Bonifacia, the chambermaid, Pepita, the butler, Truchuela, the chauffeur, Jehová, the gardener, Cándido . . . The staff was not only perfect but silent. Señor Albarrán did not need to exchange words with a single servant to have everything in its place at the correct time. He did not even need to look at them.

At nine in the evening, in pajamas, robe, and slippers, when he sat in the wingback chair in his bedroom to eat a modest light meal of foaming hot chocolate and a sweet roll, Don Luis Albarrán could anticipate a night of recuperative sleep with the spiritual serenity of having honored, for another day, the sweet memory of his loyal companion, Matilde Cousiño, a Chilean who had until the day of her death been a southern beauty with those green eyes that rivaled the cold of the South Pacific and were all that had been left to her of a body slowly defeated by the relentless advance of cancer.

Matilde: Illness only renewed her firm spirit, her character immune to any defeat. She said that Chilean women (she pronounced it "wimmen") were like that, strong and decisive. They made up for—this was her theory—a certain weak sweetness in the men of her country, so cordial until the day their treble voices turned into commanding, cruel voices. Then the woman's word would appear with all its gift for finding a balance between tenderness and strength.

They had a happy love life in bed, a "carousing" counterpoint, Don Luis would say, in two daily lives that were so serious and orderly until the illness and death of his wife left the widower momentarily disconcerted, possessed of all obligations—office and home—and bereft of all pleasures.

The staff responded. They all knew the routine. Doña Matilde Cousiño came from an old Chilean family and was trained in ruling over the estates of the south and the elegant mansions of Providencia, and she inculcated in her Mexican staff virtues with which they, the domestic crew of the Polanco district, were not unfamiliar and normally accepted. The only novelty for Don Luis was having, when he returned home, elevenses, the amiable Chilean version of British afternoon tea: cups of verbena with tea cakes, dulce de leche, and almond pastries. Don Luis told himself that this and a good wine cellar of Chilean reds were the only exotic details Doña Matilde Cousiño introduced into the mansion in Polanco. The staff continued the Chilean custom. Given Mexican schedules, however (office from ten to two, dinner from two to four, final business items from four to six), Don Luis had elevenses a little later, at seven in the evening, though this sweet custom cut his appetite for even the monastic meal he ate at nine.

Doña Matilde Cousiño, as it turned out, died on Christmas Eve, so for Don Luis, December 24 was a day of mourning, solitude, and remembrance. Between the night of the twenty-fourth and the morning of the twenty-fifth, Señor Albarrán dismissed the servants and remained alone, recalling the details of life with Matilde, perusing the objects and rooms of the house, kneeling at the bed his wife occupied at the end of her life, playing records of old Chilean tunes and Mexican boleros that choked him with romantic and sexual nostalgia, going through photograph albums, and preparing rudimentary meals with odds and ends, gringo cereals and spoonfuls of Coronado jelly. He had a sweet tooth, it was true, he saw nothing wrong in sweetening his bitterness and something sinful in stopping at a mirror hoping to see the face of his lost love, and the sorrow that ensued when he discovered only a closely shaved face, an aquiline nose, eyes with increasingly drooping lids, a broad forehead, and graying hair vigorously brushed straight back.

The doorbell rang at eight on the evening of December 24. Don Luis was surprised. The entire staff had left. The days of asking for lodgings were over, destroyed by the city's dangers, and still the voice on the other side of the door of corrugated glass and wrought iron sang the Christmas song,

> *iiiin the name of heaaaaa-ven*
> *I ask yoooou for loooodging . . .*

Don Luis, incapable of admitting his incipient deafness, approached the door, trying to make out the silhouette outlined behind the opaque panes. The voice, obviously, was a caricature of childish tones; the height of the silhouette was that of an adult.

"Who is it?"

"Guess, good guesser."

Dissolute, unruly, strewing the same destructive actions no matter where he was or whom he was with, at home or outside. The news had arrived: He was the same as always. Thirty-four forgotten years returned at one stroke, making Don Luis Albarrán's extended hand tremble as he wavered between opening the door to his house or saying to the suspect phantom,

"Go away. I never want to see you again. What do you want of me? Get away. Get away."

II

REYES ALBARRÁN HAD BEEN GIVEN that name because he was born on January 5, a holiday that, in the Latino world, celebrates the arrival of the Santos Reyes, Melchor, Gaspar, and Baltasar, bearing gifts of gold, frankincense, and myrrh to the stable in Bethlehem. Centuries before the appearance of Santa Claus, children in Mexico and Chile, Spain and Argentina, celebrated the Day of the Kings as the holiday with presents and homemade sweets, culminating in the ceremony of the rosca de reyes, the ring-shaped kings' cake inside which is hidden a little white porcelain figure of Baby Jesus.

Tradition dictates that whoever cuts the piece of cake that hides the baby is bound to give a party on the second day of the following month, February, and every month after that. Few get past the month of March. Nobody can endure an entire year of Christmas parties. The last time he saw his brother, Don Luis received from him a rosca de reyes with twelve little dolls of Baby Jesus, one next to the other. It was a treacherous invitation from Reyes to Luis: "Invite me every month, brother."

Matilde said it: "On top of everything else, he's a scrounger. I don't want to see him again. Not even as a delivery boy."

When Luis Albarrán, moved by an uncontrollable mixture of blameworthy argumentativeness, buried fraternity, seignorial arrogance, unconscious valor, but especially shameful curiosity, opened the door of his house on that December 24, the first thing he saw was the outstretched hand with the little porcelain doll held between thumb and index finger. Don Luis felt the offense of the contrast between the pulchritude of the doll and the grime of the cracked fingers, the broken nails edged in black, the shredded shirt cuff.

"What do you want, Reyes?" said Luis abruptly. With his brother, courtesy was not merely excessive. It was a dangerous invitation.

"Lodging, brother, hospitality," a voice as cracked as the fingers replied from the darkness. It was a voice broken by cheap alcohol: A stink of rum lashed the nostrils of Don Luis Albarrán like an ethylic whip.

"It isn't—" he began to say, but the other man, Reyes Albarrán, had already pushed him away to come into the vestibule. Don Luis stood to one side, almost like a doorman, and rapidly closed the door as if he feared that a tribe of beggars, drunkards, and sots would come in on the heels of his undesirable brother.

He repeated: "What do you want?"

The other man guffawed, and his Potrero rum breath floated toward the living room. "Look at me and you tell me."

Don Luis stood outside the bathroom listening to his brother singing "Amapola" in a loud off-key voice, splashing with joy and punctuating his song with paleo-patriotic observations: "Only—Veracruz—is—beautiful, howprettyismichoacán, Ay! Chihuahua! What! Apache!" as if the guest wanted to indicate that for the past three and a half decades, he had traveled the entire republic. Only because of a trace of decency, perhaps, he did not sing "Ay Jalisco, don't brag."

And if not the entire republic, Reyes had traveled—Don Luis said with alarmed discretion—its lowest, most unfortunate neighborhoods, its black holes, its spider nests, its overgrown fields of bedbugs, lice, and chancres, its maw of ashes, mud, and garbage. It was enough to look at the pile of dirty, frayed clothing riddled with holes, and its grayish tone, with no real color or form: Reyes Albarrán had left all this—the rags of wretchedness—at the bathroom door. With repugnance, the master of the house smelled his acrid armpits, the crust of his asshole, the bitter intimacy of his pubis.

He closed his eyes and tried to imagine the handsome, intelligent boy who, at the age of twenty-four, ruled over the most exclusive bar in Mexico City, the Rendez-Vous, facing the traffic circle of the Angel of Independence, when the capital had two and not twenty million inhabitants, when all the known people really did know one another and would meet at the Rendez-Vous, where, with luck, night after night, you would see one of the many celebrities who, in those days, frequented the exotic Mexican metropolis—John Steinbeck, Paulette Goddard, Aaron Copland, Virginia Hill. The so-called most transparent region, still wearing the halo of the recent glories of European exile and the distant fires of the Mexican Revolution.

Reyes Albarrán not only made cocktails. He was a cocktail. He mixed languages, references, gossip, jokes, he played the piano, he sang Agustín Lara and Cole Porter, combed his hair with pomade, imitated Gardel, introduced surprising mixtures of alcohol with irresistible names—the Manhattan, the sidecar, the Tom Collins—attempted to bring together necessary and dissimilar couples, urged homosexuals and lesbians to show themselves without complexes, impelled boys ruined by the Revolution to fall in love with girls enriched by the same event, deceived the Hungarian princess dispossessed by Communism into marrying the false rogue without a cent posing as a petro-millionaire from Tabasco. Between drinks, he imagined them all, learning on their wedding night that between the two of them—the princess and the rogue—they couldn't put two eggs in the refrigerator.

"My specialty is launching penury in pursuit of wealth," he would say, the sophisticated Reyes Albarrán with his elbow on the bar and a gin fizz in his hand.

But the clientele—*hélas!*—began to understand that the owner of the Rendez-Vous was a mocker, a gossip, a cruel and talkative man, even if he tended bar with burlesque religious solemnity, serving each drink with an "ego baptiso te whiskey sour" and closing the establishment at the hour prescribed by law with a no less mocking "Ite Bacchus est."

He loved, in other words, to humiliate his clients while pretending to protect them. But since the clients eventually saw the light, rancor and suspicion accumulated around Reyes Albarrán. He knew too many secrets, he laughed at his own mother, he could put an end to many reputations by means of gossip columns and whispered slander. They began to abandon him.

And the city was growing, the fashionable places changed like serpents shedding skin, social barriers fell, exclusive groups became reclusive or inclusive, the names of the old families no longer meant anything, those of the new families changed with each presidential term before they retired to enjoy their six-year fortunes, engagements to be married were determined by distances, the new Outer Ring dictated debuts, dates, angers, punctual loves, lost friendships . . .

Luxury and the places that were frequented moved from the Juárez district to the Zona Rosa to Avenida Masaryk, right here in the Polanco district where the shipwrecked survivor of the postwar period, the pomaded and seductive Reyes Albarrán, had been tossed up one Christmas Eve to knock on the door of his solid old brother, the punctual and industrious Don Luis Albarrán, a recent widower, undoubtedly in need of the fraternal company of the equally needy bartender who had ended as a drunkard, forgetting the golden rule: To be a good saloon keeper, you also have to be a good abstainer.

A drunkard, a pianist in an elegant boîte who ended up pounding the keys in the brothels of the Narvarte district like Hipólito el de Santa, a pomaded seducer of European princesses who ended up living at the expense of rumberas in decline, a waiter in funky holes and, with luck, dives close to the Zócalo, the Plaza Mayor where, more than once, he was found sleeping, wrapped in newspapers, awakened by the clubs of the heartless Technicolor gendarmerie of the increasingly dangerous metropolis. Cops, blue, tamarind, all of them on the take, except what could they put the bite on him for except hunger? Stumbling through the entire republic in search of luck, not finding it, stealing bus tickets and lottery tickets, the first bringing more fortune than the second, carrying him far and sinking him into being broke until the doctor in Ciudad Juárez told him, "You're no longer the man you were, Señor Albarrán. You've lived a long time. It isn't that you're sick. You're just worn out. I mean exhausted. You can't do any more. The wind's gone out of you. I see that you're over seventy. I advise you to retire. For your own good."

If some buried tenderness remained in Don Luis Albarrán toward his older brother, Reyes Albarrán (the "Don" didn't come off even as a joke), the implacable Chilean Doña Matilde Cousiño had kept him from bringing it to the surface: "That filthy beggar doesn't set foot in my house. Don't let yourself be ruled by affection, Lucho. Your brother had everything, and he threw it all away. Let him live in his shanties. He doesn't come in here. Not while I'm alive. No, Señor."

But she wasn't alive now. Though her will was. That night Don "Lucho" Albarrán felt as never before the absence of his willful wife. She would have thrown the discomfiting brother out on the street with a sonorous, very Chilean:

"Get the hell out of here, you damn ragged beggar!"

III

AS TENDS TO HAPPEN to most human beings, Don Luis Albarrán woke up in a bad mood. If sleeping is an anticipation of death, then it is a warm, comfortable, welcoming announcement. If dreaming is death, then it is the great open door of hospitality. Everything in that kingdom is possible. Everything we desire lies within reach. Sex. Money. Power. Food and drink. Imaginary landscapes. The most interesting people. Connections to celebrity, authority, mystery. Of course, an oneiric counterpart exists. One dreams of accidents. Dreams are dimensions of our circulation, and as Doña Matilde would say,

"Lucho, don't be an asshole. We're nothing but accidents of our circulation."

Except that accidents in a dream tend to be absurd. Walking naked down the street is the prototype. Or they can be mortal. Falling from the top floor of a skyscraper, like King Kong. Except at that moment the angel sent by Morpheus wakes us, the dream is interrupted, and then we give it an ugly name, *pesadilla*. Borges, said the very southern and well-read Doña Matilde, detested that terrible word and wondered why we didn't have a good word in Spanish for a bad dream, for example, *nightmare* or *cauchemar*.

Don Luis recalled these ideas of his Chilean dreamer regarding dreams, and he prayed as he was falling precisely into the arms of Morpheus:

"Get away, *pesadilla*. Welcome, *cauchemar*, hidden sea, invisible ocean of dreams, welcome, *nightmare*, nocturnal mare, mount of the darkness. Welcome to you both, drive the ugly Spanish *pesadilla* away from me."

Don Luis awoke that morning convinced that his bad mood was the usual one upon opening his eyes and that a good Mexican breakfast of spicy huevos rancheros and steaming coffee from Coatepec would be enough to return him to reality.

The newspaper carefully opened on the table by Truchuela, the butler, noisily displayed news much worse than the worst personal dream. Once again the world was on its head, and the *pesadillas, cauchemars,* or *nightmares* of the previous night seemed mere fairy tales compared to ordinary reality. Except that this morning the austere face of Truchuela, as long and sour as that of any actor cast in the role of a butler with a long, sour face, was more sour and longer than usual. And in case Don Luis didn't notice, Truchuela filled the cup to the brim with coffee and even dared to spill it.

"The Señor will please excuse me."

"What?" said a distracted Don Luis, bewitched by his effort to decipher the tongue twisters of high Mexican officials.

"Excuse me. I spilled the coffee."

No expression of Don Luis's justified what Truchuela wanted to say: "The Señor will forgive me, but the unexpected guest in the blue bedroom—"

"He is not unexpected," said Don Luis with a certain severity. "He is my brother."

"So he said," Truchuela agreed. "It was difficult for us to accept that."

"Us? How many are *you*, Truchuela?" Don Luis replied with a growing irritation, directed at himself more than at the perfect servant imported from Spain and accustomed to waiting on the superior clientele of El Bodegón in Madrid.

"We are *all of us*, Señor."

From this it appeared that Reyes, installed in the blue bedroom in less than a morning following the return of the staff, had demanded:

a) That he be served breakfast in bed. A request fulfilled by the chambermaid, Pepita, whom Reyes ordered to let him sleep postprandially (Truchuela's preferred expression) until noon before returning (Pepita) to run the water in the bath (tub) and sprinkle it with lavender salts.

b) That the cook, María Bonifacia, come up to the top floor (something she had never done) to receive orders regarding the menu to be followed not only today but for all breakfasts hereafter (marrow soup, brain quesadillas, chicken with bacon and almonds, pork in wine sauce, and also pigs' feet, everything can be used, yellow *mole*, stuffed cheese from Yucatán, smoked meat, jerked beef, and ant eggs in season.

"'Señor Don Luis eats simpler food, he isn't going to like your menu, Señor—?'

"'Reyes. Reyes Albarrán. I'm your employer's brother.'

"Yes, Señor Don Luis, he said everything 'in quotation marks,' " the butler affirmed.

"And what else?" Don Luis inquired, certain that no new petro-war of Mr. Bush's would be worse news than what came next from the mouth of Truchuela.

"He ordered that the gardener, Cándido, be told that there are no roses in his bedroom. That he is accustomed to having roses in his bedroom."

"Roses?" Don Luis said with a laugh, imagining the prickly pears that must have been the habitual landscape for his unfortunate vagabond brother.

"And he has asked Jehová the chauffeur to have the Mercedes ready at three this afternoon to take him shopping at the Palacio de Hierro."

"Modest."

"'I'm totally Palacio,' said your . . . brother?" The impassive Truchuela broke; he could contain himself no longer. "Your brother, Señor Don Luis? How can that be? That—"

"Say it, Truchuela, don't bite your tongue. That vagrant, that bum, that tramp, that beggar, that *clochard*, they exist everywhere and have a name, don't limit yourself."

"As you say, Señor." The butler bowed his head.

"Well yes, Truchuela, he is my brother. An unwelcome Christmas gift, I admit. His name is Reyes, and he will be my guest until the Day of the Kings, January 5. From now until that date—ten days—I ask you to tell the staff to treat him as a gentleman, no matter how difficult it may be for them. Put up with his insolence. Accept his whims. I'll know how to show my gratitude."

"The Señor does honor to his well-known generosity."

"All right, Truchuela. Tell Jehová to have the car ready to go to the office. And to come back for my brother at three."

"As the Señor wishes."

When he was back in the kitchen, Truchuela said, "The Señor is a model gentleman."

"He's a saintly soul," contributed the cook, María Bonifacia.

"He's nuts," said the gardener, Cándido. "Roses in January are only for the Virgin of Guadalupe. Let him be happy with daisies."

"Let him go push them up," an indignant Pepita said with a laugh. "A bum dying of hunger."

"Push them up? What, the daisies?" Cándido asked with a smile.

"Yes, but not my butt, which is what he tried to do when he asked me to dry him when he got out of the tub."

"And what did you do?" they all asked at once, except for the circumspect Truchuela.

"I told him to dry himself, dirty old man, jerk with big hands."

"He'll complain about you to the boss."

"No, he won't! He just laughed and shook his wrinkled dried-up prick with his hand. It was like the ones on those old monkeys in the zoo. 'Keep your chipotle pepper to yourself,' I said to the indecent old creep. 'Little but delicious,' sang the old son of a bitch."

"Pepita, don't risk your job," said the prudent María Bonifacia.

"I can have plenty of jobs, Doña Boni, I'm not ready to be thrown away like you."

"Respect my gray hairs, you stupid girl."

"Better if I pull them out, you miserable old woman."

The three men separated the women. Truchuela laid down the law: "Don't let this unwanted guest have his way and make us enemies. We're a staff that gets along. Isn't that true, Pepita?"

The chambermaid agreed and bowed her head. "I'm sorry, María Bonifacia."

The cook caressed Pepita's dark braided head. "My girl. You know I love you."

"So," dictated Truchuela, "we'll serve Don Reyes Albarrán. No complaints, kids. Just information. We obey the boss. But we let the boss know."

Unusually for the month of January, a downpour fell on the city, and everyone went to tend to duties except the gardener, who sat down to read the crime newspaper *Alarma!*

IV

DON LUIS ALBARRÁN had decided that the best way to dispatch his discomfiting brother was to treat him like a beloved guest. Charm him first and then dispatch him. That is: January 6, bye-bye, and if I saw you, I don't remember. This was the grand plan of the master of the house. He counted on the patience and loyalty of the servants to bring his scheme to a successful conclusion.

"I have no other recourse," he said to the spirit, accusatory from the grave, of his adored Doña Matilde.

Certainly, Don Luis tried to avoid Reyes as much as possible. But an encounter was inevitable, and the discomfiting brother took it upon himself to have his supper served in Don Luis's bedroom in order to have him captive at least once a day, in view of Don Luis's daily flights to the office (while Reyes slept until noon) or business lunches (while Reyes had himself served Pantagruelian, typically Mexican lunches) or his return from the office (while Reyes went "shopping" at the Palacio de Hierro, since he had no money and had to content himself with looking).

Until Don Luis saw Jehová come in with an outsize tower of packages which he carried up to the bedroom of *Don* Reyes. "What's that?" an irritated Don Luis inquired.

"Today's purchases," Jehová answered very seriously.

"Today's purchases? Whose?"

"Your brother's, Señor. Every day he goes shopping at the Palacio de Hierro." The chauffeur smiled sardonically. "I think he's going to buy out all their stock." He added with singular impudence: "The truth is, he doesn't buy things just for himself but for everybody."

"Everybody?" Don Luis's irritated perplexity increased.

"Sure. A miniskirt for Pepita, new gloves for the gardener, a flowered Sunday dress for Doña Boni, Wagner's operas for Truchuela, he listens to them in secret—"

"And for you?" Don Luis put on his most severe expression.

"Well, a real chauffeur's cap, navy blue with a plastic visor and gold trim. What you never bothered to give me, and that's the damn truth."

"Show some respect, Jehová!"

"As you wish, Señor," replied the chauffeur with a crooked, mischievous, irritating little smile that once would have been the prelude to dismissal. Except that Jehová was too good a chauffeur, when most had gone to drive trucks across the border in the era of NAFTA.

In any case, how did he dare?

"How nice." Don Luis smiled affably when Truchuela brought him his usual light meal of chocolate and pastries, and for Reyes, sitting now across from his brother, a tray filled with enchiladas suizas, roasted strips of chile peppers, fritters, omelets, and a couple of Corona beers.

"Sure, give it your best," replied Reyes.

"I see you're well served."

"It was time." Reyes began to chew. He was dressed in a red velvet robe, blue slippers, and a Liberty ascot.

"Time for what?"

"Time to say goodbye, Luisito."

"I repeat, time for what? Haven't I treated you like a brother? Haven't I kept my Christmas promise? You will be my guest until tomorrow, the Day of the Kings, and—"

"And then kick me out on the street?" The discomfiting brother almost choked on his laughter.

"No. To each his own life," Don Luis said in a hesitant voice.

"The fact is, I'm having a fantastic time. The fact is, my life now is here, at the side of my adored *fratellino*."

"Reyes," Don Luis said with his severest expression. "We made a deal. Until January sixth."

"Don't make me laugh, Güichito. Do you think that in a week you can wipe away the crimes of an entire life?"

"I don't know what you're talking about. We haven't seen each other in thirty years."

"That's the point. You don't keep very good accounts." Reyes swallowed a chalupa and licked the cream from his lips with his tongue. "Sixty years, I'm telling you . . . You were so solemn as a boy. The favorite son. You condemned me to second place. The clown of the house."

"You were older than me. You could have affirmed your position as firstborn. It isn't my fault if—"

"Why should I drag out the story? You were the studious one. The punctual one. The traitor. The schemer. Do you think I didn't hear you tell our father: 'Reyes does everything wrong, he's a boy with no luck, he's going to hurt us all, Papa, get him out of the house, send him to boarding school.'"

Reyes was swallowing chalupas whole. "Do you remember when we both went to Mass together every Sunday, Luisito? Ah, we were believers. It's what hurts me most. Having lost my faith. And you're to blame, little brother."

Don Luis had to laugh. "You astonish me, Reyes."

"No." Reyes laughed. "I'm the one who's astonished. You're only stupefied. You must have thought you'd never see me again."

"You're right. I don't want to see you again. On the sixth, you—"

"I what? Recover my innocence?"

Luis looked at him gravely. "When were you ever innocent?"

"Until the day you said to me: 'Asshole, we go to Mass every Sunday, but we don't believe in God, we only believe in ourselves, in our personal success; don't go around thinking Divine Providence will come to help you. Look at yourself, Reyes, so overgrown and so devout, look at your younger brother, I tell you. I go to Mass to please Papa and Mama, the family, while you, Reyes, you go because you believe in God and religion. What a joke, the younger brother is smarter than the older brother, the baby knows more than the big galoot. And what does the baby know? That you come into this world to be successful with no scruples, to beat out everybody else, to move ahead over other people's good faith or conviction or morality.' "

He took a foaming drink of beer, tilting back the bottle. "Nobody believes my story, brother. How can it be that the little brother *corrupts* the older one? Because you corrupted me, Luis. You left me with a *malignant* relationship to the world. I saw you move up, marry a rich girl, manipulate politicians, negotiate favors, and in passing rip out my innocence."

"A carouser. You had a vocation for dissipation."

"How could I believe in the good with a diabolical brother like you?"

"A tree that grows twisted—"

"God made you like that, or did you betray God Himself?"

"Soul of a delinquent—"

"Did you betray God, or did God betray you?"

Don Luis choked on a biscuit. His brother stood up to pound him on the back and didn't stop talking.

"I wanted an ordered, simple life. Your example stopped me. You moved up so quickly. Ha, like the foam on this brew. You were so greedy. You know how to use people and then throw them into the trash. Your diabolical wife gave you feudal tips. The arrogance of Chilean landowners. And you spiced up the stew with Mexican malice, fawning, climbing, betraying, using."

"Water . . ." Luis coughed.

"Ah yes, Señor." Reyes moved away the glass. "Everything in order to reach the age of sixty-five with a gorgeous house in Polanco, five—count 'em—five servants, eight board presidencies, a dead wife, and a boozing brother."

"You are what you wanted to be, a poor devil." Don Luis coughed. "I didn't force you."

"Yes." With a blow of his hand, Reyes knocked the tray of chocolate and biscuits to the floor. "Yes! You challenged me to emulate you, and I didn't know how." His eyes filled with tears. "You lent me the dough to set up a bar."

"And you got drunk making your customers drunk, you poor idiot," Don Luis replied, using his napkin to wipe the mess of chocolate and crumbs from his shirt and lap.

"I wanted to be consistent in my vices," Reyes said with misplaced pride. "Just like you."

"Pick up what you knocked down."

Reyes, smiling, obeyed. Don Luis stood, went to the desk, sat, wrote out a check, tore it from the checkbook, and offered it to Reyes.

"Take it. It's ten thousand dollars. Take the check and get out right now."

His brother took the check, tore it into pieces, and threw them in Don Luis's face. "There's no need. I can imitate your signature. Ask them in the shops. I bought everything on your signature, friend. Ask your servants. Everything I've bought has been with your checks signed by me." He brought his face and his mouthful of tortilla up to his brother's face. "You look confused. That's why I'll say it again. Signed by you." He moved away, satisfied. "It's an art I learned in order to survive."

In one hand, Reyes flapped Don Luis's checkbook like the wing of a wounded bird, and in the other, he waved a silver American Express card. "Look, brother. Life consists in our getting used to the fact that everything will go badly for us."

V

"NO, WHAT DO YOU MEAN, Don Luis, your brother is a saint. Imagine, he ordered a marble stone for my dear mother's grave in Tulancingo. I always wanted that, boss, seeing how everybody walks on a grave without a stone, nobody respects a grave marked with little stones and a couple of carnations. And now, thanks to Señor Reyes, my dear mother rests in peace and devotion. And I say to myself, María Bonifacia, God bless the boss's brother."

"Well, Señor, I've been driving your Mercedes for what? Twelve years? And at the end of the day, what do I have? Taking the bus and traveling an hour to my house. You never thought about that, did you? Well your brother did, he did. 'Go on, Jehová, here are the keys to your 1934 Renault. You have a right to your own car. What did you think? You'll never ride a bus again. Of course you won't.'"

"Imagine, boss, I go back to my village on Sunday, and they welcome me with wreaths of flowers saying thank you Cándido. You know that on the road to Xochimilco, there's water but no land. Now I have land and water, and my children can take care of cultivating flowers, thanks to the piece of land your brother gave us, that saint."

"Oh, boss, I'm sorry for the bad impression of your brother I gave you. For years in my village of Zacatlán de las Manzanas, we've been asking for a school for the girls because as soon as they're twelve, they're deflowered, as they say, and loaded down with kids, and they have to go to work in a rich man's house, like me. And now the village has a school and a gift of scholarships so the girls can keep studying until they're sixteen, and then they leave with a diploma and are secretaries or nurses and not just maids like me, and they come to their weddings pure. Your brother's so kind, Don Luisito!"

"The complete works of Wagner. Do you realize what that means, Señor Don Luis? The dream of my life. Before I'd save enough for an opera here, a bel canto selection there . . . No, damn it, begging the Señor's pardon, now the complete works of Don Ricardo, let's hope I live long enough to listen to all the CDs, a gift from your brother. Don Luis, it was a lucky day when he came to live in this house."

VI

MORNING AFTER MORNING, Don Luis Albarrán woke with his head full of good intentions. Each evening, Reyes Albarrán came with a new, bad, and worse intention.

"I'm going to imagine that you're a dream," Don Luis told him with an evil look.

"Don't hide from the world anymore, Güichito."

"I'm afraid of unfortunate people like you. They bring bad luck."

"We're brothers. Let's bury the truth in the deepest grave."

"Get out of here."

"You invited me. Be sensible."

"Sensible! You came into my house like an animal. A beast lying in ambush. You're a parasite. And you've turned all my employees into parasites."

"The parasites of a parasite."

"Leave me alone. For just one day. Please," Don Luis shouted and rose to his feet, exasperated.

"What are you afraid of?" replied Reyes very calmly.

"Unfortunate people. The evil eye. Unfortunate people like you bring us bad luck. Bad luck is contagious. A jinx."

Reyes laughed. "So you have the soul of a Gypsy and a minstrel . . . Look, your cynicism toward religion, which I reminded you of the other day, came with a price, Luisito. Since we didn't perform the penance of the Church, we have to perform the penance of life."

"Penance? You filthy bum, I don't—"

"Do you even look at your servants? Have you smelled your cook up close, saturated with the aromas of your damn huevos rancheros for breakfast? Tell me the truth, brother, how many people *do you know*? How many people have you *really* gotten close to? Do you live only for the next administrative board?"

Reyes took Luis by the shoulders and shook him violently. The businessman's glasses fell off. With one hand, Reyes tousled Luis's hair.

"Answer me, junior."

Don Luis Albarrán stammered, stunned by bewilderment, injury, impotence, the mental flash that told him, "Everything I can do against my brother, my brother can do against me."

"And even worse, Luisito. Who looks at you? Really, who *looks* at you?" Reyes let Luis go with a twisted smile, half boastful, half melancholy. "You live in the ruin of yourself, brother."

"I'm a decent man." Don Luis composed himself. "I don't harm anybody. I'm compassionate."

"Compassion doesn't harm anybody?" The discomfiting brother pretended to be amazed. "Do you believe that?"

"No. Not anybody."

"Compassion insults the one who receives it. As if I didn't know that."

"Cynic. You've shown compassion to all my servants."

"No. I've given them what each one deserved. I think that's the definition of justice, isn't it?" Reyes walked to the door of the bedroom and turned to wink at his brother. "Isn't it?"

VII

"PERMIT ME TO EXPRESS my astonishment to you, Don Luis."

"Tell me, Truchuela."

"Your brother—"

"Yes."

"He's gone."

Don Luis sighed. "Did he say what time he'd be back?"

"No. He said, 'Goodbye, Truchuela. Today is the Day of the Kings. The vacation's over. Tell my brother. I'm leaving forever, goodbye.' "

"Did he take anything with him?" Don Luis asked in alarm.

"No, Señor. That's the strangest part. He was wearing his beggar's clothes. He wasn't carrying suitcases or anything." The butler coughed. "He smelled bad."

"Ah yes. He smelled bad. That will be all, Truchuela."

That was all, Don Luis Albarrán repeated to himself as he slowly climbed the stairs to his bedroom. Everything would return to its normal rhythm. Everything would go back to what it had been before.

He stopped abruptly. He turned and went down to the first floor. He walked into the kitchen with a firm step. He realized he was seeing it for the first time. The servants were eating. They got to their feet. Don Luis gestured for them to sit down. Nobody dared to. Everything would go on as it always had.

Don Luis exchanged glances with each servant, one by one, "Do you ever look at your servants?" and he saw that nothing was the same. His employees' glances were no longer the same, the boss said to himself. How did he know if, in reality, he had never looked at them before? Precisely for that reason. They were no longer invisible. The routine had been broken. No, it wasn't a lack of respect. Looking at each one, he was certain about that.

It was a change in spirit that he could not distinguish but that he felt with the same physical intensity as a blow to the stomach. In a mysterious way, the routine of the house, though it would be repeated punctually from then on, from then on would no longer be the same.

"Will you all believe me?" said Don Luis in a very quiet voice.

"Señor?" inquired the butler, Truchuela.

"No, nothing." Don Luis shook his head. "What are you preparing in the oven, Bonifacia?"

"La rosca de reyes, Señor. Did you forget that today is the Day of the Kings?"

He left the kitchen on the way to his bedroom, on the way to his routine, on the way to his daily penance.

"From now on, everything will put me to the test," he said as he closed the door, looking at the photograph of the beautiful Chilean Matilde Cousiño out of the corner of his eye.

Yes, he said to himself, yes, I have known love.

He slept peacefully again.

2006

THE OLD MAN

Amado Nervo

I

EVERY TIME THE WHEEL of the year—bristling with more spikes than even Saint Catherine's wheel, judging by the grief it brings us—completes a full turn, and the first frost covers the tranquil and melancholy Valley of Mexico with a crystalline mantle, I remember a story my old wet nurse, Donaciana, would tell, December after December, in the month's final days, in a corner of the warm smoky kitchen.

My country does not have poetic traditions. The French old Noel, whose affable smile lights up the virgin forest of a beard that has received so many winter snows, has never been mentioned in those parts; despite the proximity to the Yankees, Santa Claus has never appeared in those valleys of mine with his load of gifts. The soft, intimate poetry of the burning hearth holding a crackling log is totally alien to those modest homes. As a result, children do not put their little shoes, and their excitement, at the edge of a genial fire, and they do not wake up surrounded by toys. A few Germans, most certainly expatriates, who have for years done business in those areas and who brought their prestigious traditions with them, stay up late on the 24th of December, surrounded by their children, gathered around a marvelous tree; even so, that lovely custom has not taken hold where I am from. The toy-giving tree does not grow in my tropics: it is a northern tree, a tree for the cold, a tree of boreal scents, a tree from unknown mountains, on the peaks of which snow is always sleeping.

Thus, the only things that distinguished the season and that continue to distinguish my memories of the end of the year were: the litanies of the Saints recited at the church, which my mother took us to, holding us by the hand; the ice on the fragrant hills; and my nurse's tale.

Around the 28th of December, my nurse would start telling us about an old man, very old, who was dying. On the 29th, the old man was frailer still; by the 30th, unable to stay on his feet, he would get into bed . . .

On the 31st, the story's appeal for us would intensify. During prayers, we would gather around my nurse, eyes wide, ears pricked, a nest of ineffable curiosity, in a smoky corner of the kitchen, and as a pot burbled on the stove and the enormous striped cat wove around the fire, we would ask, once every minute, endlessly: "The old man, Nana, what about the old man?"

"He's very old and very sick," replied Donaciana mysteriously. "He's dying in a bed covered in frost . . . Soon the priest will come to take his last confession. They've already sent for him."

"What does the old man look like, Nana?"

"Ah! He's so skinny he looks like a bundle of bones . . . His eyes are very blue, but they're very cloudy now."

"Like my *abuelita*'s?"

"Like your abuelita's . . . His face is marked with wrinkles, like the furrows in the fields now covered in ice. He's very short, and he has a walking stick to lean on; but he won't be getting up from his bed!"

"Doesn't the old man have children?"

"He has one, just one, who will be born right at midnight; red-cheeked and very handsome, about to born . . ."

That would leave us fully satisfied, because then we knew, as a matter of course, that the old man was the year that was ending, and his son was the year that was about to arrive.

As night drew closer, the old man's condition grew worse; his breath began to rattle . . . ; they helped him to a good death . . . But we were never there for his death or for the birth of his son, and the reason was simple: we went to bed early.

For many years, that monotonous story was invariably repeated every

December. I grew up, and despite my elementary books, kneaded and rolled out at the private school where the good women made us spell out the basic notions of geography and cosmography, I continued thinking of the year coming to a close as a blue-eyed, flaxen-haired old man on his deathbed, and of the new year as a plump and impish baby, son of the year before . . .

II

LATER I LEARNED MANY THINGS: I learned that Earth is the third planet in our system, a star as bright as Venus; that it spins around the sun for a length of time that is almost identical to that of our calendar year; that its youth is eternal in comparison to the flicker of our own existence; that the winter ice harbors under its mantle the hidden germination of the spring to follow; that everything is reborn, ceaselessly; that one day we will be old and lie down to sleep in a dark cradle, stretched out and melancholy, and never again see morning's blush, or the golden harvests of midday, or the gloomy austerity of twilight. But this will not put an end to the world's reproductive forces; and spring will return year after year, and people will continue to entrust their hopes to January, to reap December's crop of sorrow; and children will laugh like they always have, even when we can no longer hear them; and adolescent couples will seek out each other's mouths for a kiss and look for each other's eyes to gaze deeply, even when we can no longer see them; and the scents and soft heat of day, and the silver-plated enigmas of night, will continue to unfurl, even when we can no longer sense them . . .

I learned that time is but another subjectivity, like space; that the pulse of the universe will go on *in aeternum*; that the sun, cooling, will become a planet; that the old planet will disintegrate and fall into the furnace of another sun and that, out of the nebula condensing the world that is ending, there is a divine and eternal path of strength and resurrection and love; that the longest human life of which there is memory is not as long as the life of a star; that the shortest, apparently, travels but a centimeter in the heavens . . .

I learned, in short, that it is not time that passes, but we who pass . . .

III

BUT I HAVE NOT FORGOTTEN the old man of yore, the old man with eyes as blue as that of my bride, whom I kissed so many times; with hair as white as my bride's silken skin, the heat of which would overwhelm my heart when, hand in hand, we walked down the road, wanting to come across the last thought of afternoon in sunset's forehead . . . I have not forgotten the old man, who was more furrowed than land tilled for sowing and covered in December by ice . . .

No, I have not forgotten the old man, dying; and now that he is turning to crawl into bed, now that he is being helped to a good death, now that I can witness his last breath—because I am no longer made to turn in early!—I ask him with a sad smile: "Tell me: What will he bring, your son, the plump baby who is about to be born?" And the old man replies: "Hopes and dreams!"

"And what will he leave me when his breath rattles like yours, good old man with the blue eyes?"

And the old man replies, sweetly: "Hopes and dreams, too . . . Hopes and dreams . . ."

1906

THE TWO CHRISTMASES

Carlos Monsiváis

Christmas, that great family holiday of the West, is the gathering that can't be avoided, an occasion for debatable humor and overflowing love, a time for reunions, for promoting good cheer and demonstrations of charitable spirit. In Latin America, Christmas was once a day steeped in tradition, with dinners opulent as can be, dueling nativity scenes and trees, religious services in joyous remembrance, the utopian idea of imminent reunification (for those once joined at the hip, the chance to see each other again is no small thing).

The positivist Auguste Comte put it lucidly: "Nothing is destroyed until it is replaced"; and over the last century and a half, even if the essence (faith) has endured, the traditions have been subject to constant replacement.

In the December 31, 1842 issue of the newspaper *El Siglo XIX*, Guillermo Prieto begins his Christmas *crónica* in a rather impassioned way: "Be sharp, pen of mine; it is December 24, and noisy bells are announcing Mass: midnight Mass. To Mass," and he refers to the sacred place's new decorations: " . . . they fill the church with original devotions: capes and cloth caps, cover them in wool and slippers, blankets and textiles, everything coordinates with the temple of the Lord." And the revelry takes over: The sober Confiteor Deo is heard, an intrusive reed whistle announces the *incarnatus*, and then to the audience's delight, the zeal of those present, and general jubilation, the festive bandolóns burst in; the low strings of the bass raise up that philharmonic world, the children's tuba toots, hands shake tambourines and rattles, and a certain worldly spirit is communicated to the Christian audience, lifting the spirits of the crowd and rejuvenating them.

To the rhythm of some charming little signal: the acolyte without a censer; the surplices too, and everyone with their merry faces, recalling perhaps the patterns and the exuberance with which, in other places, skillful dancers move to the rhythms being played.

Among the differences evident between yesteryear and now are the real and the declared reasons for joy. In the first decades of the twentieth century, the reason was still the Birth of the Lord. Now in most cases, *Nochebuena* (Christmas Eve) is celebrated on Christmas Day—which is a real pleasure, because Christmas Eve has already passed and continues to take place, iteratively.

The religious sentiments have been preserved, with some dilution perhaps, but the goal of the holiday does vary. For example, Prieto describes an idyllic situation: whether it's the predisposition of the spirit, or the communicative nature of delight, or the power of tradition, joy transcends, everywhere; thunderous fireworks climb upward, furrowing the air, producing fantastic ephemeral lights in the dark emptiness; the accents of the music and the voices in the chorus of litanies can be heard; visible through the crack in the half-open door of a neighborhood house are streamers hanging from the ceiling, curtains, and lamps in the corridors, a hubbub and a buzzing crowd . . .

External causes (the beginning of the Christian era) give way to internal motivations (the family reunion).

"In this corner, fresh from New York—the tree!"

The crónica writers of the nineteenth century contended that Christmas is not a holiday of the people or even of families, but of the community of believers, and only modernity has definitively altered this belief. The first split originated in the threat occasioned by "heretical" North America, and that is why, in the 1930s, the Christmas tree caused a scandal, as the adoption of that pernicious symbol was "a renunciation of our roots." Twenty or twenty-five years later, the tree has become a modern-day custom in Mexico City, the nativity scenes as a creative practice having disappeared without warning (no one has the time or the resources), returning only as an aesthetic tradition. And the tree, despite the objections of the environmentally aware, is the decorative element punctuating the arrangement of the modern family's home.

"And I wish you a Merry Christmas." Among the many shifts are those in the season's songs. The traditional carols have been eclipsed in favor of the international repertoire, with "Silent Night" leading the charge.

Taste originates from repetition, and in the last few decades, acoustic taste has become a conditioned response; "White Christmas" and "Santa Claus Is Coming to Town" are accepted without a fuss, and by the end of the twentieth century, the melodic repertoire of Christmas was basically derived from the traditions and commercials of North America. Christmas Eve may come, but it's more bilingual every year.

And one day we will depart this place and consume no more. In recent years, the celebration of Christmas has been thoroughly disrupted. For me, there are at least two Christmases. The first is the one of Christian affirmations, family, and mutual good will; the second is the apotheosis of consumption, the triumph of obligatory mall visits that have become elements of communal life.

Many of the traditions of family Christmas are also being lost or misplaced. For example: the practice of *posadas* processions has diminished due to household financial constraints and the latest trends. The Christmas of consumption finds its Yuletide spirit shaped by television advertisements. Jingle bells, jingle bells, jingle all the way . . . and in the malls, people are wearing coats and scarves that make them look like extras in a gringo movie, waiting for "Rudolph" the red-nosed reindeer; *Santaclós* is coming to town tonight, and *en la blanca Navidad*, the tree tops glisten.

Not only are tastes and traditions being imported. Something else is happening too: the holiday habits of Americanization, those of the consumption nation, the new continent, are being assimilated here.

I will not dwell on Americanization, an inexhaustible topic, and instead just comment on one of those scarcely noted changes in mentality. In the beginning, the empire's sum of advantages is imposed, along with admiration for its efficiency and technological supremacy; then, people and groups do not quite renounce their identity, but mix and mingle it with the other identity, the one proclaimed in North America. Even if things are now merely Mexican in a new way, the great family holiday unfolds entirely differently. Christmas Eve remains, but with far too many modifications.

2003

MOSES AND GASPAR

Amparo Dávila

The train arrived at about six o'clock on a cold, wet November morning. The fog was so thick it was almost impossible to see. I was wearing my coat collar up and my hat shoved down around my ears, but still the fog penetrated all the way to my bones. Leonidas lived in a neighborhood far from the center of town, on the sixth floor of a modest apartment building. Everything — the staircase, the hallways, the rooms — was invaded by the fog. As I climbed the stairs I thought I was approaching eternity, an eternity of mist and silence. Leonidas, my brother, when I reached your door, I thought I would die of grief! I had come to visit you the year before, during my Christmas break. "We'll have turkey stuffed with olives and chestnuts, an Italian Spumante, and dried fruit," you said, radiant with happiness, "Moses, Gaspar, let's celebrate!" Those days were always so festive. We drank a lot and talked about our parents, about the apple *pasteles*, the evenings by the fire, the old man's pipe and his absent, down-cast gaze that we couldn't forget, the winter sweaters that Mamá knitted for us, that aunt on our mother's side who buried all her money and died of hunger, the professor of mathematics with his starched collars and bow ties, the girls from the drugstore we took to the movies on Sundays, those films we never watched, the handkerchiefs covered in lipstick that we had to throw away . . . In my grief, I had forgotten to ask the concierge to unlock the apartment. I had to wake her up; she climbed the stairs half asleep, dragging her feet. There were Moses and

Gaspar, but when they saw me they fled in terror. The woman said she'd been feeding them twice a day — and yet, to me, they looked all skin and bones.

"It was horrible, Señor Kraus. I saw him with my own eyes, here in this chair, slumped over the table. Moses and Gaspar were lying at his feet. At first I thought they were all asleep — they were so quiet! But it was already late and Señor Leonidas would always wake up early and go out to buy food for Moses and Gaspar. He ate downtown, but he always fed them first; I suddenly realized that . . ."

I made some coffee and tried to pull myself together before going to the funeral parlor. Leonidas, Leonidas, how could it be? Leonidas, so full of life, how could you be lying stiff in a cold refrigerator drawer?

The funeral was at four in the afternoon. It was raining and the cold was intense; everything was gray, with only black hats and umbrellas interrupting the monotony; raincoats and faces blurred into the fog and drizzle. A fair number of people had come to the funeral: coworkers, perhaps, and a few friends. I navigated within the bitterest of dreams. I wanted this day to be over, to wake up without that knot in my throat, without the mind-numbing sense of being torn apart. An old priest said a prayer and blessed the grave. Afterward, someone I didn't recognize handed me a cigarette and took me by the arm in a familiar way, offering his condolences. We left the cemetery; Leonidas stayed behind, forever.

I walked alone, aimless, beneath the persistent, dull rain. Hopeless, crippled in my soul. My only happiness, the one great affection that tied me to this earth, had died with Leonidas. We had been inseparable since childhood, but for years the war kept us apart. Finding each other again, after the fighting and the solitude, was the greatest joy of our lives. We were the only two left in the family: nevertheless, we soon realized that we ought to live separate lives, and that's what we did. During those years, each of us had acquired his own customs, habits, and absolute independence. Leonidas found a job as a bank teller; I went to work for an insurance company as an accountant. During the week, both of us dedicated ourselves to our own work or solitude; but Sundays we always spent together. How happy we were then! I assure you, we both looked forward to that day of the week.

Sometime later they moved Leonidas to another city. He could have quit and looked for another position. His way, though, was always to accept things with exemplary serenity. "It's useless to resist; we could circle around a thousand times and always end up where we began . . ." "We've been so happy, there had to be a catch; happiness comes at a price . . ." This was his philosophy and he bore it calmly and without defiance. "There are some things you can't fight against, my dear José . . ."

Leonidas went away. For a time, his absence was more than I could bear; then slowly we began to organize our solitary lives. We wrote to each other once or twice a month. I spent my vacations with him and he came to see me during his. And so our lives went by . . .

Night had fallen by the time I returned to his apartment. The cold was more intense and it was still raining. I had a bottle of rum under my arm, which I'd bought from a store that I'd found open. The apartment was utterly dark and freezing. I stumbled my way in, switched on the light, and connected the heater. I uncorked the bottle nervously, with clumsy, trembling hands. There, at the table, in the last spot that Leonidas had occupied, I sat down to drink, to vent my sorrow. At least I was alone and didn't have to hold back or hide my pain from anyone; I could weep and cry and . . . Suddenly I felt eyes behind me. I jumped out of the chair and spun around: there were Moses and Gaspar. I had forgotten all about them, but there they were, staring at me — with hostility? With mistrust? I couldn't tell. But their gaze was terrible. In the moment I didn't know what to tell them. I felt hollowed out and absent, as though I were outside myself and had lost the power to think. Besides, I didn't know how much they understood . . . I went on drinking . . . Then I realized that they were both silently weeping. The tears dripped from their eyes and fell to the floor; they wept with no expression and without a sound. At around midnight, I made coffee and prepared them a bit of food. They wouldn't touch it, only went on crying disconsolately . . .

Leonidas had arranged all of his affairs. Perhaps he had burned his files, because I didn't find a single one in the apartment. As far as I knew, he'd sold his furniture on the pretext that he was going away; it was all going to be picked up the next day. His clothes and other personal effects were carefully packed in two trunks labeled with my name. His savings and the money from the furniture had been deposited in the bank, also in my name. Everything was in order. The only things he left me in charge of were his burial and the care of Moses and Gaspar.

AT AROUND FOUR in the morning we departed for the train station: our train left at five fifteen. Moses and Gaspar had to travel, to their obvious disgust, in the baggage car; they weren't allowed to ride with the passengers — not at any price. What a grueling trip! I was physically and morally spent. I'd gone four days and four nights without sleeping or resting, ever since the telegram had arrived with the news that Leonidas was dead. I tried to sleep during the trip but managed only to doze. In the stations where the train made longer stops, I went to check on Moses and Gaspar and see if they wanted something to eat. The sight of them wounded me. They seemed to be recriminating me for their situation. "You know it's not my fault," I repeated each time, but they couldn't, or didn't want to, understand. It was going to be very difficult for me to live with them: they'd never taken to me, and I felt uncomfortable in their presence, as though I were always being watched. How unpleasant it had been to find them in his house that past summer! Leonidas evaded my questions and begged me in the warmest terms to love them and put up with them. "The poor things deserve to be loved," he told me. That vacation was exhausting and violent, even though the mere fact of seeing Leonidas filled me with happiness. He had stopped coming to visit me, since he couldn't leave Moses and Gaspar alone. The next year — the last time I saw Leonidas — everything went more normally. I didn't like Moses and Gaspar and I never would, but they no longer made me so uneasy. I never found out how they came to live with Leonidas . . . Now they were with me, a legacy, an inheritance from my unforgettable brother.

It was after eleven at night when we arrived at my house. The train had been delayed more than four hours. The three of us were completely worn out. All that I had to offer Moses and Gaspar was some fruit and a little bit of cheese. They ate without enthusiasm, watching me suspiciously. I threw some blankets down in the living room so they could sleep, then shut myself in my room and took a sleeping pill.

The next day was Sunday, which meant I was spared from having to go to work — not that I could have gone. I had planned to sleep late, but I began to hear noises at the first light of dawn. It was Moses and Gaspar: they had already woken up and were pacing from one side of the apartment to the other. They came up to my bedroom door and stood there, pressing themselves against it, as if they were trying to see through the keyhole, or maybe just listening for the sound of my breathing to see whether I was still asleep. Then I remembered that Leonidas fed them every morning at seven. I had to get up and find them something to eat.

What hard and arduous days those were after Moses and Gaspar came to live in my house! I was used to waking up a little before eight, making coffee, and leaving for the office at eight thirty, since the bus took half an hour and my job started at nine. With Moses and Gaspar there, my whole life was thrown into chaos. I had to wake up at six to buy milk and other groceries, then make their breakfast — they ate punctually at seven, according to their habit. If I was late, they grew furious, which frightened me because I didn't know just how far their anger might go. I had to clean up the apartment every day, because with them there, I always found everything out of place.

But what tortured me the most was their hopeless grief. The way they searched for Leonidas and stood waiting for him at the door. Sometimes, when I came home from work, they ran jubilantly to greet me, but as soon as they saw it was me, they put on such disappointed, suffering faces that I broke down and wept along with them. This was the only thing we shared. There were days when they hardly got up; they spent all day lying there, listless, taking no interest in anything. I would have liked to know what they were thinking then. The fact was that I hadn't explained anything to them when I went to pick them up. I don't know if Leonidas had said something to them, or if they knew . . .

MOSES AND GASPAR had been living with me for almost a month when I finally realized the serious problem they were going to create in my life. For several years I'd had a romantic relationship with the cashier of a restaurant where I often ate. Our friendship began in a straightforward way, because I've never been the courting kind. I simply needed a woman, and Susy solved that problem. At first, we saw each other only now and then. Sometimes a month or two would pass in which we did nothing more than greet each other at the restaurant with a nod of the head, like mere acquaintances. I would go on living calmly for a while, without thinking about her, then all at once I'd feel old and familiar symptoms of anxiety, sudden rages, and melancholy. Then I'd look up Susy and everything would return to normal. After a while, almost habitually, Susy came to visit once a week. When I went to pay the check for dinner, I'd say, "Tonight, Susy." If she was free — since she did have other engagements — she'd answer, "I'll see you tonight," otherwise it was, "Not tonight, but tomorrow if you like." Susy's other engagements didn't bother me; we owed each other nothing and didn't belong to each other. Advancing in years and abundant in flesh, she was far from being a beauty; but she smelled good and always wore silk underwear with lace trim, which had a notable influence on my desire. I've never managed to recall even one of her dresses, but her intimate combinations I remember well. We never spoke while making love; instead, the two of us both seemed lost inside ourselves. When we said goodbye, I always gave her some money. "You're very generous," she would say in satisfaction; but beyond this customary gift, she never asked me for anything. The death of Leonidas interrupted our routine relations. More than a month passed before I went looking for Susy. I'd spent the whole month in the most hopeless grief, which I shared with no one but Moses and Gaspar, who were just as much strangers to me as I was to them. Finally one night I waited for Susy at the corner outside the restaurant, as usual, and we went up to my apartment. Everything happened so quickly that I was able to piece it together only afterward. When Susy entered the bedroom, she saw Moses and Gaspar there, cornered in fright under the sofa. She turned so pale that I thought she was going to faint, then she screamed like a lunatic and dashed down the stairs. I ran after her and had a hard time calming her down. After that unfortunate accident, Susy never came back to my apartment. When I wanted to see her, I had to rent a hotel room, which threw off my budget and annoyed me.

THE INCIDENT WITH SUSY was only the first in a series of calamities.

"Señor Kraus," the concierge said to me one day, "all of the tenants have come to complain about the unbearable noise that comes from your apartment as soon as you leave for the office. Please do something about it, because there are people like Señorita X or Señor A who work at night and need to sleep during the day."

I was taken aback and didn't know what to think. Overwhelmed as they were by the loss of their owner, Moses and Gaspar lived in silence. At least that's how they were when I was in the apartment. Seeing them so downcast and diminished, I said nothing — it seemed too cruel. Besides, I had no evidence against them . . .

"I'm sorry to bother you again, but this can't go on," the concierge told me a few days later. "As soon as you leave, they start dumping all the stuff in the kitchen on the floor, they throw the chairs around, they move the beds and all the furniture. And the screams, the screams, Señor Kraus, are horrible; we can't take it anymore, and it lasts all day until you come home."

I decided to investigate. I asked permission at the office to take a few hours off. I came home at noon. The concierge and all the tenants were right. The whole building seemed about to collapse with the unbearable racket that was coming from my apartment. I opened the door. Moses was on top of the stove, bombarding Gaspar from above with pots and pans, while Gaspar ran around dodging the projectiles, screaming and laughing like a maniac. They were so engaged in their game that they didn't notice me there. The chairs were over-turned, the pillows flung onto the table, onto the floor . . . When they saw me, they froze.

"I can't believe what I'm seeing!" I shouted in rage. "I've gotten complaints from all the neighbors and I refused to believe them. How ungrateful! This is how you repay my hospitality and honor your master's memory? His death is ancient history to you, it happened so long ago you don't even feel it — all you care about are your games. You little demons, you ingrates!"

When I finished, I realized they were lying on the floor in tears. I left them there and returned to the office. I felt bad all the rest of the day. When I came home in the afternoon, the house had been cleaned up and they were hiding in the closet. I felt terrible pangs of remorse; I felt that I'd been too hard on those poor creatures. Maybe, I thought, they don't know that Leonidas is never coming back, maybe they think that he's only gone on a trip and that one day he'll return — maybe the more they hope, the less it hurts. And I've destroyed the only thing that makes them happy . . . But my remorse ended soon enough; the next day I learned that they had been at it again: the noise, the screams . . .

Not long after this I was evicted by court order, and so we began moving from place to place. A month here, another there, another there . . . One night, I was feeling worn down and depressed by the series of disasters that had befallen me. We had a small apartment consisting of a tiny living room, a kitchen, a bath-room, and one bedroom. I decided to turn in for the night. When I went into the bedroom, I saw that they were asleep on my bed. Then I remembered: the last time I'd visited Leonidas, on the night I arrived, I noticed that my brother was improvising two beds in the living room. "Moses and Gaspar sleep in the bedroom, we'll have to make ourselves comfortable out here," he said, rather self-consciously. At the time, I couldn't understand how Leonidas could possibly bend to the will of those two miserable creatures. Now I understood . . . From that day on, they occupied my bed and there was nothing I could do about it.

I had never been close with my neighbors, because I found the idea exhausting. I preferred my solitude, my independence. Still, we greeted each other on the stairs, in the hallways, in the street . . . With the arrival of Moses and Gaspar, all of that changed. In every apartment we stayed in — which was never for very long — the neighbors developed a fierce hatred for me. There always came a point when I became afraid to enter the building or to leave my apartment. Returning home late at night, after having been with Susy, I thought I might be assaulted. I heard doors opening as I went by, or footsteps behind me, furtive, silent, someone's breath . . . When I finally entered my apartment I would be bathed in cold sweat and trembling from head to toe.

Soon I had to give up my job; I was afraid that if I left them alone, they might be killed. There was such hatred in everyone's eyes! It would have been easy to break into the apartment; or the concierge might even have opened it himself, because he hated them, too. I quit my job, and my only source of income was the bookkeeping I could do at home, small accounts that weren't enough to live on. I left early in the morning, when it was still dark, to buy the food I cooked myself. I didn't go out again except to turn in or pick up the ledgers, and I did this as fast as I could, almost running, so that I wouldn't be out long. I stopped seeing Susy; I no longer had the time or the money. I couldn't leave them alone, either by day or by night, and she refused ever to come back to my apartment. Bit by bit I began to run through my savings, and then through the money Leonidas had left me. I was earning a pittance, not even enough for food, much less the constant moving from place to place. So I decided to go away.

With the money I had left, I bought a small old farm outside the city and a few essential pieces of furniture. It's an isolated house, half in ruins. There the three of us will live, far from everything but safe from ambush and assault, tightly joined by an invisible bond, by a stark, cold hatred and an indecipherable design.

Everything is ready for our departure — everything, or rather, the little there is to bring with us. Moses and Gaspar are also awaiting the moment when we will set off. I can tell by their air of anxiety. I think they're satisfied. Their eyes shine. If only I could know what they're thinking! But no, I would be afraid to plumb the shadowy mystery of their being. Silently they approach me, as if they wanted to sniff out my mood or, perhaps, to find out what I'm thinking. But I know they can sense it, they must, for it shows in their joy, in the air of triumph that fills them whenever I feel a longing to destroy them. And they know I can't, they know I'll never fulfill my most ardent desire. They enjoy it . . . How many times would I have killed them if it had been up to me! Leonidas, Leonidas, I can't even judge your decision! You loved me, no doubt, as I loved you, but your death and your legacy have destroyed my life. I don't want to think or believe that you coldly condemned me or planned my ruin. No, I know it is something stronger than we are. I don't blame you, Leonidas: even if this is your doing, it was meant to be: "We could circle around a thousand times and always end up where we began."

1959

CHRISTMAS NIGHT

Amado Nervo

Shepherds, shepherdesses,
Eden is unbarred.
Hear the sounding voices!
Born today Our Lord.

Born today is Christ:
radiant are the skies,
lowly straw, the nest
where the birdling lies.

Noble ox, behold
baby shivering!
Warm breath in the cold,
robe the infant king!

Angel wings and voices
soar through every part:
heaven's host rejoices,
heaven, earth … and heart.

CHRISTMAS NIGHT

Hear the sounding chorus,
all the troop of them,
loud extol Christ's glories,
born in Bethlehem!

Come, you band of shepherds,
flocking from the fold:
see the son of David
long ago foretold!

LIKE WATER FOR CHOCOLATE

Laura Esquivel

INGREDIENTS:

1 can of sardines
1/2 chorizo sausage
1 onion
oregano
1 can of chiles serranos
10 hard rolls

PREPARATION:

Take care to chop the onion fine. To keep from crying when you chop it (which is so annoying!), I suggest you place a little bit on your head. The trouble with crying over an onion is that once the chopping gets you started and the tears begin to well up, the next thing you know you just can't stop. I don't know whether that's ever happened to you, but I have to confess it's happened to me, many times. Mama used to say it was because I was especially sensitive to onions, like my great-aunt, Tita.

Tita was so sensitive to onions, any time they were being chopped, they say she would just cry and cry; when she was still in my great-grandmother's belly her sobs were so loud that even Nacha, the cook, who was half-deaf, could hear them easily. Once her wailing got so violent that it brought on an early labor. And before my great-grandmother could let out a word or even a whimper, Tita made her entrance into this world, prematurely, right there on the kitchen table amid the smells of simmering noodle soup, thyme, bay leaves, and cilantro, steamed milk, garlic, and, of course, onion. Tita had no need for the usual slap on the bottom, because she was already crying as she emerged; maybe that was because she knew then that it would be her lot in life to be denied marriage. The way Nacha told it, Tita was literally washed into this world on a great tide of tears that spilled over the edge of the table and flooded across the kitchen floor.

That afternoon, when the uproar had subsided and the water had been dried up by the sun, Nacha swept up the residue the tears had left on the red stone floor. There was enough salt to fill a ten-pound sack—it was used for cooking and lasted a long time. Thanks to her unusual birth, Tita felt a deep love for the kitchen, where she spent most of her life from the day she was born.

When she was only two days old, Tita's father, my great-grandfather, died of a heart attack and Mama Elena's milk dried up from the shock. Since there was no such thing as powdered milk in those days, and they couldn't find a wet nurse anywhere, they were in a panic to satisfy the infant's hunger. Nacha, who knew everything about cooking—and much more that doesn't enter the picture until later—offered to take charge of feeding Tita. She felt she had the best chance of "educating the innocent child's stomach," even though she had never married or had children. Though she didn't know how to read or write, when it came to cooking she knew everything there was to know. Mama Elena accepted her offer gratefully; she had enough to do between her mourning and the enormous responsibility of running the ranch—and it was the ranch that would provide her children the food and education they deserved—without having to worry about feeding a newborn baby on top of everything else.

From that day on, Tita's domain was the kitchen, where she grew vigorous and healthy on a diet of teas and thin corn gruels. This explains the sixth sense Tita developed about everything concerning food. Her eating habits, for example, were attuned to the kitchen routine: in the morning, when she could smell that the beans were ready, at midday, when she sensed the water was ready for plucking the chickens, and in the afternoon, when the dinner bread was baking, Tita knew it was time for her to be fed.

Sometimes she would cry for no reason at all, like when Nacha chopped onions, but since they both knew the cause of those tears, they didn't pay them much mind. They made them a source of entertainment, so that during her childhood Tita didn't distinguish between tears of laughter and tears of sorrow. For her laughing was a form of crying.

Likewise for Tita the joy of living was wrapped up in the delights of food. It wasn't easy for a person whose knowledge of life was based on the kitchen to comprehend the outside world. That world was an endless expanse that began at the door between the kitchen and the rest of the house, whereas everything on the kitchen side of that door, on through the door leading to the patio and the kitchen and herb gardens was completely hers—it was Tita's realm.

Her sisters were just the opposite: to them, Tita's world seemed full of unknown dangers, and they were terrified of it. They felt that playing in the kitchen was foolish and dangerous. But once, Tita managed to convince them to join her in watching the dazzling display made by dancing water drops dribbled on a red-hot griddle.

While Tita was singing and waving her wet hands in time, showering drops of water down on the griddle so they would "dance," Rosaura was cowering in the corner stunned by the display. Gertrudis, on the other hand, found this game enticing, and she threw herself into it with the enthusiasm she always showed where rhythm, movement, or music were involved. Then Rosaura had tried to join them—but since she barely moistened her hands and then shook them gingerly, her efforts didn't have the desired effect. So Tita tried to move her hands closer to the griddle. Rosaura resisted, and they struggled for control until Tita became annoyed and let go, so that momentum carried Rosaura's hands onto it. Tita got a terrible spanking for that, and she was forbidden to play with her sisters in her own world. Nacha became her playmate then. Together they made up all sorts of games and activities having to do with cooking. Like the day they saw a man in the village plaza twisting long thin balloons into animal shapes, and they decided to do it with sausages. They didn't just make real animals, they also made up some of their own, creatures with the neck of a swan, the legs of a dog, the tail of a horse, and on and on.

Then there was trouble, however, when the animals had to be taken apart to fry the sausage. Tita refused to do it. The only time she was willing to take them apart was when the sausage was intended for the Christmas rolls she loved so much. Then she not only allowed her animals to be dismantled, she watched them fry with glee.

The sausage for the rolls must be fried over very low heat, so that it cooks thoroughly without getting too brown. When done, remove from the heat and add the sardines, which have been deboned ahead of time. Any black spots on the skin should also have been scraped off with a knife. Combine the onions, chopped chiles, and the ground oregano with the sardines. Let the mixture stand before filling the rolls.

Tita enjoyed this step enormously; while the filling was resting, it was very pleasant to savor its aroma, for smells have the power to evoke the past, bringing back sounds and even other smells that have no match in the present. Tita liked to take a deep breath and let the characteristic smoke and smell transport her through the recesses of her memory.

It was useless to try to recall the first time she had smelled one of those rolls—she couldn't, possibly because it had been before she was born. It might have been the unusual combination of sardines and sausages that had called to her and made her decide to trade the peace of ethereal existence in Mama Elena's belly for life as her daughter, in order to enter the De la Garza family and share their delicious meals and wonderful sausage.

On Mama Elena's ranch, sausage-making was a real ritual. The day before, they started peeling garlic, cleaning chiles, and grinding spices. All the women in the family had to participate: Mama Elena; her daughters, Gertrudis, Rosaura, and Tita; Nacha, the cook; and Chencha, the maid. They gathered around the dining room table in the afternoon, and between the talking and the joking the time flew by until it started to get dark. Then Mama Elena would say:

"That's it for today."

For a good listener, it is said, a single word will suffice, so when they heard that, they all sprang into action. First they had to clear the table; then they had to assign tasks: one collected the chickens, another drew water for breakfast from the well, a third was in charge of wood for the stove. There would be no ironing, no embroidery, no sewing that day. When it was all finished they went to their bedrooms to read, say their prayers, and go to sleep. One afternoon, before Mama Elena told them they could leave the table, Tita, who was then fifteen, announced in a trembling voice that Pedro Muzquiz would like to come and speak with her . . .

After an endless silence during which Tita's soul shrank, Mama Elena asked:

"And why should this gentleman want to come talk to me?"

Tita's answer could barely be heard:

"I don't know."

Mama Elena threw her a look that seemed to Tita to contain all the years of repression that had flowed over the family, and said:

"If he intends to ask for your hand, tell him not to bother. He'll be wasting his time and mine too. You know perfectly well that being the youngest daughter means you have to take care of me until the day I die."

With that Mama Elena got slowly to her feet, put her glasses in her apron, and said in a tone of final command:

"That's it for today."

Tita knew that discussion was not one of the forms of communication permitted in Mama Elena's household, but even so, for the first time in her life, she intended to protest her mother's ruling.

"But in my opinion . . ."

"You don't have an opinion, and that's all I want to hear about it. For generations, not a single person in my family has ever questioned this tradition, and no daughter of mine is going to be the one to start."

Tita lowered her head, and the realization of her fate struck her as forcibly as her tears struck the table. From then on they knew, she and the table, that they could never have even the slightest voice in the unknown forces that fated Tita to bow before her mother's absurd decision, and the table to continue to receive the bitter tears that she had first shed on the day of her birth.

Still Tita did not submit. Doubts and anxieties sprang to her mind. For one thing, she wanted to know who started this family tradition. It would be nice if she could let that genius know about one little flaw in this perfect plan for taking care of women in their old age. If Tita couldn't marry and have children, who would take care of her when she got old? Was there a solution in a case like that? Or are daughters who stay home and take care of their mothers not expected to survive too long after the parent's death? And what about women who marry and can't have children, who will take care of them? And besides, she'd like to know what kind of studies had established that the youngest daughter and not the eldest is best suited to care for their mother. Had the opinion of the daughter affected by the plan ever been taken into account? If she couldn't marry, was she at least allowed to experience love? Or not even that?

Tita knew perfectly well that all these questions would have to be buried forever in the archive of questions that have no answers. In the De la Garza family, one obeyed—immediately. Ignoring Tita completely, a very angry Mama Elena left the kitchen, and for the next week she didn't speak a single word to her.

What passed for communication between them resumed when Mama Elena, who was inspecting the clothes each of the women had been sewing, discovered that Tita's creation, which was the most perfect, had not been basted before it was sewed.

"Congratulations," she said, "your stitches are perfect—but you didn't baste it, did you?"

"No," answered Tita, astonished that the sentence of silence had been revoked.

"Then go and rip it out. Baste it and sew it again and then come and show it to me. And remember that the lazy man and the stingy man end up walking their road twice."

"But that's if a person makes a mistake, and you yourself said a moment ago that my sewing was . . ."

"Are you starting up with your rebelliousness again? It's enough that you have the audacity to break the rules in your sewing."

"I'm sorry, Mami. I won't ever do it again."

With that Tita succeeded in calming Mama Elena's anger. For once she had been very careful; she had called her "Mami" in the correct tone of voice. Mama Elena felt that the word *Mama* had a disrespectful sound to it, and so, from the time they were little, she had ordered her daughters to use the word *Mami* when speaking to her. The only one who resisted, the only one who said the word without the proper deference was Tita, which had earned her plenty of slaps. But how perfectly she had said it this time! Mama Elena took comfort in the hope that she had finally managed to subdue her youngest daughter.

Unfortunately her hope was short-lived, for the very next day Pedro Muzquiz appeared at the house, his esteemed father at his side, to ask for Tita's hand in marriage. His arrival caused a huge uproar, as his visit was completely unexpected. Several days earlier Tita had sent Pedro a message via Nacha's brother asking him to abandon his suit. The brother swore he had delivered the message to Pedro, and yet, there they were, in the house. Mama Elena received them in the living room; she was extremely polite and explained why it was impossible for Tita to marry.

"But if you really want Pedro to get married, allow me to suggest my daughter Rosaura, who's just two years older than Tita. *She* is one hundred percent available, and ready for marriage."

At that Chencha almost dropped right onto Mama Elena the tray containing coffee and cookies, which she had carried into the living room to offer don Pascual and his son. Excusing herself, she rushed back to the kitchen, where Tita, Rosaura, and Gertrudis were waiting for her to fill them in on every detail about what was going on in the living room. She burst headlong into the room, and they all immediately stopped what they were doing, so as not to miss a word she said.

They were together in the kitchen making Christmas Rolls. As the name implies, these rolls are usually prepared around Christmas, but today they were being prepared in honor of Tita's birthday. She would soon be sixteen years old, and she wanted to celebrate with one of her favorite dishes.

"Isn't that something? Your ma talks about being ready for marriage like she was dishing up a plate of enchiladas! And the worse thing is, they're completely different! You can't just switch tacos and enchiladas like that!"

Chencha kept up this kind of running commentary as she told the others—in her own way, of course—about the scene she had just witnessed. Tita knew Chencha sometimes exaggerated and distorted things, so she held her aching heart in check. She would not accept what she had just heard. Feigning calm, she continued cutting the rolls for her sisters and Nacha to fill.

It is best to use homemade rolls. Hard rolls can easily be obtained from a bakery, but they should be small; the larger ones are unsuited for this recipe.

After filling the rolls, bake for ten minutes and serve hot. For best results, leave the rolls out overnight, wrapped in a cloth, so that the grease from the sausage soaks into the bread.

When Tita was finishing wrapping the next day's rolls, Mama Elena came into the kitchen and informed them that she had agreed to Pedro's marriage—to Rosaura.

Hearing Chencha's story confirmed, Tita felt her body fill with a wintry chill: in one sharp, quick blast she was so cold and dry her cheeks burned and turned red, red as the apples beside her. That overpowering chill a lasted a long time, and she could find no respite, not even when Nacha told her what she had overheard as she escorted don Pascual Muzquiz and his son to the ranch's gate. Nacha followed them, walking as quietly as she could in order to hear the conversation between father and son. Don Pascual and Pedro were walking slowly, speaking in low, controlled, angry voices.

"Why did you do that, Pedro? It will look ridiculous, your agreeing to marry Rosaura. What happened to the eternal love you swore to Tita? Aren't you going to keep that vow?"

"Of course I'll keep it. When you're told there's no way you can marry the woman you love and your only hope of being near her is to marry her sister, wouldn't you do the same?"

Nacha didn't manage to hear the answer, Pulque, the ranch dog, went running by, barking at a rabbit he mistook for a cat.

"So you intend to marry without love?"

"No, Papa, I am going to marry with a great love for Tita that will never die."

Their voices grew less and less audible, drowned out by the crackling of dried leaves beneath their feet. How strange that Nacha, who was quite hard of hearing by that time, should have claimed to have heard this conversation. Still, Tita thanked Nacha for telling her—but that did not alter the icy feelings she began to have for Pedro. It is said that the deaf can't hear but can understand. Perhaps Nacha only heard what everyone else was afraid to say. Tita could not get to sleep that night; she could not find the words for what she was feeling. How unfortunate that black holes in space had not yet been discovered, for then she might have understood the black hole in the center of her chest, infinite coldness flowing through it.

Whenever she closed her eyes she saw scenes from last Christmas, the first time Pedro and his family had been invited to dinner; the scenes grew more and more vivid, and the cold within her grew sharper. Despite the time that had passed since that evening, she remembered it perfectly: the sounds, the smells, the way her new dress had grazed the freshly waxed floor, the look Pedro gave her . . . That look! She had been walking to the table carrying a tray of egg-yolk candies when she first felt his hot gaze burning her skin. She turned her head, and her eyes met Pedro's. It was then she understood how dough feels when it is plunged into boiling oil. The heat that invaded her body was so real she was afraid she would start to bubble—her face, her stomach, her heart, her breasts—like batter, and unable to endure his gaze she lowered her eyes and hastily crossed the room, to where Gertrudis was pedaling the player piano, playing a waltz called "The Eyes of Youth." She set her tray on a little table in the middle of the room, picked up a glass of Noyo liquor that was in front of her, hardly aware of what she was doing, and sat down next to Paquita Lobo, the De la Garzas' neighbor. But even that distance between herself and Pedro was not enough; she felt her blood pulsing, searing her veins. A deep flush suffused her face and no matter how she tried she could not find a place for her eyes to rest. Paquita saw that something was bothering her, and with a look of great concern, she asked:

"That liquor is pretty strong, isn't it?"

"Pardon me?"

"You look a little woozy, Tita. Are you feeling all right?"

"Yes, thank you."

"You're old enough to have a little drink on a special occasion, but tell me, you little devil, did your mama say it was okay? I can see you're excited—you're shaking—and I'm sorry but I must say you'd better not have any more. You wouldn't want to make a fool of yourself."

That was the last straw! To have Paquita Lobo think she was drunk. She couldn't allow the tiniest suspicion to remain in Paquita's mind or she might tell her mother. Tita's fear of her mother was enough to make her forget Pedro for a moment, and she applied herself to convincing Paquita, any way she could, that she was thinking clearly, that her mind was alert. She chatted with her, she gossiped, she made small talk. She even told her the recipe for this Noyo liquor which was supposed to have had such an effect on her. The liquor is made by

EXCERPT FROM **LIKE WATER FOR CHOCOLATE**

soaking four ounces of peaches and a half pound of apricots in water for twenty-four hours to loosen the skin; next, they are peeled, crushed, and steeped in hot water for fifteen days. Then the liquor is distilled. After two and a half pounds of sugar have been completely dissolved in the water, four ounces of orange-flower water are added, and the mixture is stirred and strained. And so there would be no lingering doubts about her mental and physical well-being, she reminded Paquita, as if it were just an aside, that the water containers held 2.016 liters, no more and no less.

So when Mama Elena came over to ask Paquita if she was being properly entertained, she replied enthusiastically.

"Oh yes, perfectly! You have such wonderful daughters. Such fascinating conversation!"

Mama Elena sent Tita to the kitchen to get something for the guests. Pedro "happened" to be walking by at that moment and he offered his help. Tita rushed off to the kitchen without a word.

His presence made her extremely uncomfortable. He followed her in, and she quickly sent him off with one of the trays of delicious snacks that had been waiting on the kitchen table.

She would never forget the moment their hands accidentally touched as they both slowly bent down to pick up the same tray.

That was when Pedro confessed his love.

"Senorita Tita, I would like to take advantage of this opportunity to be alone with you to tell you that I am deeply in love with you. I know this declaration is presumptuous, and that it's quite sudden, but it's so hard to get near you that I decided to tell you tonight. All I ask is that you tell me whether I can hope to win your love."

"I don't know what to say . . . give me time to think."

"No, no, I can't! I need an answer now: you don't have to think about love, you either feel it or you don't. I am a man of few words, but my word is my pledge. I swear that my love for you will last forever. What about you? Do you feel the same way about me?"

"Yes!"

Yes, a thousand times. From that night on she would love him forever. And now she had to give him up. It wasn't decent to desire your sister's future husband.

She had to try to put him out of her mind somehow, so she could get to sleep. She started to eat the Christmas Roll Nacha had left out on her bureau, along with a glass of milk; this remedy had proven effective many times.

Nacha, with all her experience, knew that for Tita there was no pain that wouldn't disappear if she ate a delicious Christmas Roll. But this time it didn't work. She felt no relief from the hollow sensation in her stomach. Just the opposite, a wave of nausea flowed over her. She realized that the hollow sensation was not hunger but an icy feeling of grief. She had to get rid of that terrible sensation of cold. First she put on a wool robe and a heavy cloak. The cold still gripped her. Then she put on felt slippers and another two shawls. No good. Finally she went to her sewing box and pulled out the bedspread she had started the day Pedro first spoke of marriage. A bedspread like that, a crocheted one, takes about a year to complete. Exactly the length of time Pedro and Tita had planned to wait before getting married. She decided to use the yarn, not to let it go to waste, and so she worked on the bedspread and wept furiously, weeping and working until dawn, and threw it over herself. It didn't help at all. Not that night, nor many others, for as long as she lived, could she free herself from that cold.

1989

THE TRAGEDY OF THE TOY

Luis Gonzaga Urbina

By now it has become common, and because it is common nobody thinks about it, the plaster figurine, the contours of which I will follow for a few lines: a boy between six and eight years old, in extravagant clothes, the doublet and the hose so close-fitting they have been absorbed into the soft curves of that Tanagra angel; his hands are lifted to his face to hide a pained and angry pout. He has been surprised by the artist with his fists about to touch his shut, wrinkled eyelids. Upright, his legs together, in an acrobatic pose, the child tips his head, from which a tumbler's hat has just been doffed and on which remains, resting on the forehead, a floury lock of hair. The remnants of laughter on his lips are broken-winged like a wounded hummingbird in the pearly cup of a magnolia. A flash of joy has just snapped shut its bright fan in this likeness of a Raphaelesque *bambino*. In that comically sorry physiognomy are the traces of fleeting satisfactions, the last kisses left by naive elation on the sturdy boy's round cheeks. All of that amusing visage's features indicate the abruptness of the unexpected turn of events: those features had been harmonizing pleasantly on a face contracted with the taut sinews of laughter when, violently impelled by a sudden irritant, they were forced to undo their expression. No matter, they are accustomed to transitions: they take their orders from the fickle soul of a little boy full of whims and caprices. But why, so swift, the

Olympic ire and the elusive pain crumpling that childish brow and truncating the corners of his mouth, the harsh lines of that ample cheek? Ah, I see! Below, on a plinth, next to the pointed clogs, is a broken-legged Pulcinella, its jingling hump sunk into the plaster by the force of the fall; it is gasping with laughter—opening the toothless mouth under its Bourbon nose—at the little boy's banal vexation. "Clumsy!" it seems to say to him.

The sun is laughing too, somewhere between touched and mirthful, stroking the milky whiteness of the figurine. "Don't cry, silly!" it tells him.

A NUMBER OF YEARS AGO, when I stopped, I do not remember where or why, to look for a moment at the figurine, I was struck by the impression of a refined melancholy, which now comes to mind every afternoon, evoked by the display windows on Calle de Plateros. The first thing that I thought then, looking at the little boy whose enjoyment had been set upon by fate, was a sentence that encloses, like a slatted box, the tightly wound thread, subtle like a strand of light, of an airy and frivolous philosophy, of the sort we contemplative nervous types so appreciate: the toy is poking fun!

Indeed: this broken-legged Pulcinella is a symbol. Its name is Love, its name is Hope, its name is Ideals, its name is Faith, depending on the situation. Who has not once been that clumsy child, that plaster figurine, who after a fumble, a careless touch, a flap of wind, was forced to watch the toy that once entertained him fall: a belief, an illusion, a dream, all of this that is really one thing, taking on different names as we go through our lives; that, in our childhood bedrooms, is the halo of our guardian angel; in our youthful delusions is the shattering of triumph's glory or of a bride's promise; and on the cold bed of old age is the yearning for a friendly touch and the mournful pursuit of rest? We had been content with seeing in our arms, according to our whims, a woman, an abundance, a conviction, a longing. For an instant we were loved, we were powerful, we were fortunate. And we went through the world dressed extravagantly like the little boy. We woke the echoes of sleep with the noise of our laughter—a frenzied chorus of naked nymphs. We believed in miracles, in the laurel crown, in the swearing of oaths. We frolicked with our Pulcinella, we shook it furiously to make it jingle, to kindle curiosity, and make envy well up. There goes—we shouted—a lover, a believer, a poet! Make way for the blessed one!

All of a sudden—how did it happen?—the toy fell from our hands, and we were left in a comical position, standing before the perversely cheerful crowd, wearing a pained and angry grimace, while, below, on the churned and muddy ground, that grotesque toy, hope, illusion, desire, laughed with the eternal irritating mockery of soulless things!

FOR FIVE AFTERNOONS I have watched an army of children flap into the markets, the stores, the toy shops, the stands of the Plaza Mayor, in search of a shiny orb, a pine branch, a porcelain bauble, a clay shepherd, a splendid piñata decked in tinsel and ribbons.

The display windows are more fantastical than ever, colorful and diaphanous, like the citadels of lore. Behind the glass, as if through the transparent gauze of dreams, one can see intricate castles of bonbons, glass mountains in gift baskets, blooming forests of stearic candles. Under the triumphal arches made of hay, the motley Christmas procession passes: the Holy Family with its heavenly guard of angels, their wings spread and swords drawn; the Three Kings' ponderous caravan next to the palm trees on the oasis and the gray cistern from which the camels drink, slow and weary; the pastoral band of pan flutes and pipes between the snowy flock of sheep and the herd of pensive cows; and the delicious anachronism, the enchanting and confused procession of Egyptian astrologers, Roman centurions, and medieval princes. In the back, the vivid kaleidoscopic stars, the cherubs' rosy flesh, the Swiss chalets, the points of whose weathervanes are scratching at the tangles of virgin silver in the frost. The imagination of the children is intoxicated by all these wonders, and their pupils drink in, tirelessly, the floating lights—red, violet, blue, green, like the plumage of dead birds in a motionless lake—of the shop windows' electric clarity. The little ones invade the avenue, running, sliding, escaping, like a gaggle of Tom Thumbs, lost in the forest of our legs.

This is the month of cold and snow; there are no festivities on the roofs as in May, or luminous tragedies in the sky as in August. Juliet would not have heard, on these evenings, the nightingale singing from beneath the phosphorescent foliage of the pomegranate tree, nor would Paul and Virginie have been able to seek shade beneath the chiseled crowns of the ash trees; but there are royal parties in new hearts, receptions in the courts of pure spirits, floral games and tournaments in sparkling fantasies. Everything sharpens and is purified in December: the clouds, the stars, the volcanoes, and dreams. It is the white month. Theo carved his ancient filigree, his symphony of silvery whiteness, while thinking about a winter morning. That is why it is the month of children and that is why Jesus chose it for his birth. So much in nature possesses that inviolate nuance, which is mixed and caressed. Fog tends to settle on the snowy crests of the mountain range: the hands of grandchildren caress the strands of white hair on their grandparents' heads.

These days are meant for innocent delights. Childish ambitions go mad. The toy shops—the lavish Babylons—are sacked by a battalion of children. There they go in unruly platoons, with bellicose expressions, raising their agitated little arms, singing their strange war songs made up of babbling and shrieks . . . They never surrender: they storm the bonbon forts, sweep through columns of dolls, destroy polychrome barricades made up of toys, desiring everything they see and wanting to wrap their hands around everything. They are insatiable.

And when the booty has been distributed, they leave with the proud vessels of victors and content smiles. I watch them walk away escorted by the satisfied honor guard of mothers, and, a strange obsession, I cannot stop thinking about the little plaster boy, set upon by fate in the middle of his delight. How many of these children will shortly have pained and angry pouts on their faces!

So much effort spent, so much energy exhausted, just for Pulcinella or Harlequin or Pierrot to fall and break!

I help them, I keep them from stumbling, I ask permission with my gaze from the mothers, and I approach them to set them right so that they can hold their trinkets properly. The ingrates look at me like I am an intruder; they wrinkle their brows and resist. I am a meddler, a bother. Of course I am smiling impassively as they throw their tantrums. I feel that I am committing a beautiful act. Poor things! It is important to help them prolong the joy of triumph and avoid the bitterness of the fall. Let them enjoy, let them get their fill. Tomorrow they will forget Harlequin and want Colombina instead. It is never too late for desire. And from toy to toy, they will arrive at adolescence, at adulthood, that is, they will become oversized children, and then Pulcinella's fall from their hands will be inevitable; and as they weep, anguished, over their untimely misfortune, they will see how the broken-legged toy—Love, Hope, Faith—laughs from the floor, gasps with laughter, at the clumsiness and suffering of the unlucky one. How searing the sarcasm with which we are contemplated by broken ideals! They fall, useless; no longer will they charm us; but, even fallen, they maintain their perpetual ironic hilarity in the face of our pain, our bitterness, our disenchantment. In vain, we bring our spasmodic hands to our eyes; in vain, we ask for mercy and comfort. We end up alone like the plaster figurine. At our feet, destroyed by the blow of the fall, lies ungrateful love, faded daydreams, lifeless ideals. Nevertheless, Pulcinella laughs. The toy is poking fun.

1896

THREE WISE GUYS

Sandra Cisneros

The big box came marked DO NOT OPEN TILL XMAS, but the mama said not until the Day of the Three Kings. Not until *Dia de los Reyes*, the sixth of January, do you hear? That is what the mama said exactly, only she said it all in Spanish. Because in Mexico where she was raised, it is the custom for boys and girls to receive their presents on January sixth, and not Christmas, even though they were living on the Texas side of the river now. Not until the sixth of January.

Yesterday the mama had risen in the dark same as always to reheat the coffee in a tin saucepan and warm the breakfast tortillas. The papa had gotten up coughing and spitting up the night, complaining how the evening before the buzzing of the insects had kept him from sleeping. By the time the mama had the house smelling of oatmeal and cinnamon, the papa would be gone to the fields, the sun already tangled in the trees, and the *urracas* screeching their rub-ber-screech cry. The boy Ruben and the girl Rosalinda would have to be shaken awake for school. The mama would give the baby Gilberto his bottle and then she would go back to sleep before getting up again to the chores that were always waiting. That is how the world had been.

But today the big box had arrived. When the boy Ruben and the girl Rosalinda came home from school, it was already sitting in the living room in front of the television set that no longer worked. Who had put it there? Where had it come from? A box covered with red paper with green Christmas trees and a card on top that said "Merry Christmas to the Gonzalez Family. Frank, Earl, and Dwight Travis. P.S. DO NOT OPEN TILL XMAS." That's all.

Two times the mama was made to come into the living room, first to explain to the children and later to their father how the brothers Travis had arrived in the blue pickup, and how it had taken all three of those big men to lift the box off the back of the truck and bring it inside, and how she had had to nod and say thank-you thank-you thank-you over and over because those were the only words she knew in English. Then the brothers Travis had nodded as well, the way they always did when they came and brought the boxes of clothes, or the turkey each November, or the canned ham on Easter, ever since the children had begun to earn high grades at the school where Dwight Travis was the principal.

But this year the Christmas box was bigger than usual. What could be in a box so big? The boy Ruben and the girl Rosalinda begged all afternoon to be allowed to open it, and that is when the mama had said the sixth of January, the Day of the Three Kings. Not a day sooner.

It seemed the weeks stretched themselves wider and wider since the arrival of the big box. The mama got used to sweeping around it because it was too heavy for her to push in a corner. But since the television no longer worked ever since the afternoon the children had poured iced tea through the little grates in the back, it really didn't matter if the box obstructed the view. Visitors that came inside the house were told and told again the story of how the box had arrived, and then each was made to guess what was inside.

It was the *comadre* Elodia who suggested over coffee one afternoon that the big box held a portable washing machine that could be rolled away when not in use, the kind she had seen in her Sears Roebuck catalog. The mama said she hoped so because the wringer washer she had used for the last ten years had finally gotten tired and quit. These past few weeks she had had to boil all the clothes in the big pot she used for cooking the Christmas tamales. Yes. She hoped the big box was a portable washing machine. A washing machine, even a portable one, would be good.

But the neighbor man Cayetano said, What foolishness, comadre. Can't you see the box is too small to hold a washing machine, even a portable one. Most likely God has heard your prayers and sent a new color TV. With a good antenna you could catch all the Mexican soap operas, the neighbor man said. You could distract yourself with the complicated troubles of the rich and then give thanks to God for the blessed simplicity of your poverty. A new TV would surely be the end to all your miseries.

Each night when the papa came home from the fields, he would spread newspapers on the cot in the living room, where the boy Ruben and the girl Rosalinda slept, and sit facing the big box in the center of the room. Each night he imagined the box held something different. The day before yesterday he guessed a new record player. Yesterday an ice chest filled with beer. Today the papa sat with his bottle of beer, fanning himself with a magazine, and said in a voice as much a plea as a prophecy: air conditioner.

But the boy Ruben and the girl Rosalinda were sure the big box was filled with toys. They had even punctured it in one corner with a pencil when their mother was busy cooking, but they could see nothing inside but blackness.

Only the baby Gilberto remained uninterested in the contents of the big box and seemed each day more fascinated with the exterior of the box rather than the interior. One afternoon he tore off a fistful of paper, which he was chewing when his mother swooped him up with one arm, rushed him to the kitchen sink, and forced him to swallow handfuls of lukewarm water in case the red dye of the wrapping paper might be poisonous.

When Christmas Eve finally came, the family Gonzalez put on their good clothes and went to Midnight Mass. They came home to a house that smelled of tamales and *atole*, and everyone was allowed to open one present before going to sleep. But the big box was to remain untouched until the sixth of January.

On New Year's Eve the little house was filled with people, some related, some not, coming in and out. The friends of the papa came with bottles, and the mama set out a bowl of grapes to count off the New Year. That night the children did not sleep in the living room cot as they usually did, because the living room was crowded with big-fannied ladies and fat-stomached men sashaying to the accordion music of the dwarf twins from McAllen. Instead the children fell asleep on a lump of handbags and crumpled suit jackets on top of the mama and the papa's bed, dreaming of the contents of the big box.

Finally, the fifth of January. And the boy Ruben and the girl Rosalinda could hardly sleep. All night they whispered last-minute wishes. The boy thought perhaps if the big box held a bicycle, he would be the first to ride it, since he was the oldest. This made his sister cry until the mama had to yell from her bedroom on the other side of the plastic curtains, Be quiet or I'm going to give you each the stick, which sounds worse in Spanish than it does in English. Then no one said anything. After a very long time, long after they heard the mama's wheezed breathing and the papa's piped snoring, the children closed their eyes and remembered nothing.

THE PAPA WAS ALREADY in the bathroom coughing up the night before from his throat when the urracas began their clownish chirping. The boy Ruben awoke and shook his sister. The mama, frying the potatoes and beans for breakfast, nodded permission for the box to be opened.

With a kitchen knife the boy Ruben cut a careful edge along the top. The girl Rosalinda tore the Christmas wrapping with her fingernails. The papa and the mama lifted the cardboard flaps and everyone peered inside to see what it was the brothers Travis had brought them on the Day of the Three Kings.

There were layers of balled newspaper packed on top. When these had been cleared the boy Ruben looked inside. The girl Rosalinda looked inside. The papa and the mama looked.

This is what they saw: the complete Britannica Junior Encyclopaedia, twenty-four volumes in red imitation leather with gold-embossed letters, beginning with Volume I, Aar–Bel and ending with Volume XXIV, Yel–Zyn. The girl Rosalinda let out a sad cry, as if her hair was going to be cut again. The boy Ruben pulled out Volume IV, Ded–Fem. There were many pictures and many words, but there were more words than pictures. The papa flipped through Volume XXII, but because he could not read English words, simply put the book back and grunted.

What can we do with this? No one said anything, and shortly after, the screen door slammed.

Only the mama knew what to do with the contents of the big box. She withdrew Volumes VI, VII, and VIII, marched off to the dinette set in the kitchen, placed two on Rosalinda's chair so she could better reach the table, and put one underneath the plant stand that danced.

When the boy and the girl returned from school that day they found the books stacked into squat pillars against one living room wall and a board placed on top. On this were arranged several plastic doilies and framed family photographs. The rest of the volumes the baby Gilberto was playing with, and he was already rubbing his sore gums along the corners of Volume XIV.

The girl Rosalinda also grew interested in the books. She took out her colored pencils and painted blue on the eyelids of all the illustrations of women and with a red pencil dipped in spit she painted their lips and fingernails red-red. After a couple of days, when all the pictures of women had been colored in this manner, she began to cut out some of the prettier pictures and paste them on loose-leaf paper.

One volume suffered from being exposed to the rain when the papa improvised a hat during a sudden shower. He forgot it on the hood of the car when he drove off. When the children came home from school they set it on the porch to dry. But the pages puffed up and became so fat, the book was impossible to close.

Only the boy Ruben refused to touch the books. For several days he avoided the principal because he didn't know what to say in case Mr. Travis were to ask how they were enjoying the Christmas present.

On the Saturday after New Year's the mama and the papa went into town for groceries and left the boy in charge of watching his sister and baby brother. The girl Rosalinda was stacking books into spiral staircases and making her paper dolls descend them in a fancy manner.

Perhaps the boy Ruben would not have bothered to open the volume left on the kitchen table if he had not seen his mother wedge her name-day corsage in its pages. On the page where the mama's carnation lay pressed between two pieces of Kleenex was a picture of a dog in a spaceship. FIRST DOG IN SPACE the caption said. The boy turned to another page and read where cashews came from.

And then about the man who invented the guillotine. And then about Bengal tigers. And about clouds.

All afternoon the boy read, even after the mama and the papa came home. Even after the sun set, until the mama said time to sleep and put the light out.

In their bed on the other side of the plastic curtain the mama and the papa slept. Across from them in the crib slept the baby Gilberto. The girl Rosalinda slept on her end of the cot. But the boy Ruben watched the night sky turn from violet. To blue. To gray. And then from gray. To blue. To violet once again.

1990

CARMEN AND PABLO

Ignacio Manuel Altamirano

As soon as the priest finished speaking to me, he was approached by the same older woman who had called him aside when we first arrived in town. Behind her was a very beautiful young woman, perhaps the most beautiful in all the village. I examined her closely, as I supposed her to be the heroine of the love story the priest had told me would unfold that night, and she was.

She was about twenty years old, tall, pale, slim, and striking, like a reed from those mountains. She was wearing an exquisite blouse adorned with lace, as is the style in this country, and dark silk petticoats; over her chest was a red silk scarf, and she was wrapped in a light shawl—also made of silk—with a long purple fringe. In addition, she was wearing gold earrings and pretty silk shoes, and a strand of coral adorned her throat. In short, the young woman was evidently the daughter of well-to-do parents. That elegant outfit of a highland virgin made her even more lovely in my eyes, and for an instant she looked like the idyllic Ruth of the Bible, or like the bride in the *Song of Solomon*.

The young woman had lowered her eyes and blushing face; but when she lifted her head to greet us, I was able to admire her velvety black eyes edged with long lashes, as well as her rose-colored cheeks, her delicate nose, and her fresh red lips. She was very pretty!

What sorrows could this captivating highlander possibly have? I was about to find out, and I was certainly very curious.

The older woman drew close to the priest and said:

"Brother, you promised us that Pablo would come . . . but he is not here!" The woman concluded her sentence in a pained way.

"No, he is not here!" repeated the young woman, and two plump tears rolled down her cheeks.

But the priest hastened to respond.

"My daughters, I did everything I could, and I had his word; perhaps he is among the other boys?"

"No, señor, he is not," the young woman replied. "I was searching for him with my eyes, and I did not see him."

"But, Carmen, my daughter," the mayor added. "There is no need to be discouraged. If the brother priest has said it will be so, you will speak with Pablo."

"Yes, uncle; but he told me it would be today, and I wanted it to be thus, for as you recall, it has been three years since they took him away, and since I believe myself to be responsible, I wished to ask his forgiveness today . . . The poor thing has suffered enough!"

"My friend," I said to the priest. "Might you be able to tell me what sorrow torments this beautiful girl and why she wishes to see this person? You had promised to tell me, and my curiosity is impatient."

"Oh! It is quite simple," the priest answered. "And I do not believe they would mind. It is a very simple story, one I will recount to you in two ways, because I know it through this girl and through the young man in question." Turning to the older woman and Carmen, he added, "Sit, please, my daughters, as I tell my good captain the story." The women sat down next to the mayor.

"Pablo was a young orphan in this town who had been in the care of an elderly aunt since he was a child. She died four years ago. The boy was diligent, courageous, daring, and good-natured, which is why the town's young people loved him; but he fell hopelessly in love with this girl Carmen, the niece of the good mayor, and one of the most virtuous young women in the entire region.

"Carmen did not return Pablo's affections, whether due to her most prudent of upbringings, which made her timid in matters of love, or due to what I deemed more likely, her alarm at the flightiness of the young man's character, prone as he was to courtships, having already had several girlfriends whom he left for the slightest of motives.

"But Carmen's shyness only served to stoke Pablo's love, which was already deep, and which he could not and did not try to tame.

"He followed the girl everywhere, though not to the point of pestering her with inopportune displays. He gathered the most splendid, exquisite flowers from the mountain, and went every morning to place them at the entrance of Carmen's house, and the girl would find these beautiful bouquets when she woke up, divining of course whose hands had placed them there. But it was all in vain: Carmen remained shy and pretended not to understand that she was the object of the young man's passion. After dwelling for some time on his futile efforts, he became discouraged, and perhaps trying to forget, he went down a dark path, a very dark path.

"He stopped working, contenting himself with earning enough to eat, and gave himself over to drink and disarray. After that point, that young man who had been so sensible before, so hardworking, who could have been faulted for nothing but being somewhat flighty, became a lost soul. Lazy, fond of alcohol, irritable, rowdy, and daring as he was, he began to regularly disturb the peace in this town, which had always been tranquil, and on more than one occasion, his scandals and brawls struck consternation into the hearts of the town's inhabitants, and kept the authorities busy. In short, he was insufferable, and naturally he attracted the ill will of the neighbors, and, with that, growing coldness from Carmen, who, if she pitied his fate, gave no signs of intending to change it by granting him her affection.

"It was around then that I arrived in the town, and as was to be expected, I sought the acquaintance of all the neighbors. The good mayor here, who was also the mayor then, gave me the most truthful reports, and of course I was glad to hear of only good people whose good habits would make it easy for me to fulfil my duties. But the mayor, with deep regret, told me he had but one poor report to add to the good ones he had communicated to me, about an orphan boy who had been so diligent and sensible but was now very lost, and was in fact leading the other boys his age gravely astray. I said to the mayor that I would take account of the poor young man and endeavor to bring him to reason.

"Indeed, I called on him, spoke with him in friendship, gave him excellent advice; he was moved to be treated in this way, but told me that his affliction had no remedy, and he had decided it was better to go into exile so as to cease being the target of the town's antagonism; but that it was difficult for him to change his behavior.

"The obstinacy of Pablo, whose background I understood, made me feel sorry for him, because he revealed to me a passionate and energetic character for which obstacles, far from spurring him on, made him feel discouraged, and that discouragement turned into desperation. In the end, my efforts were in vain.

"I knew very well what Pablo needed to return to how he had been before. Some hope in his love would have accomplished what not even the most eloquent appeal could have; but that hope was not forthcoming, nor was it likely to be forthcoming, as with every passing day, Carmen hardened against him, on top of which her mother and her uncle the mayor constantly disparaged the boy's conduct, and often said that they would rather see their daughter and niece dead than hear her express the least affection for him.

"Furthermore, because the town's most well-to-do young men all wanted Carmen's hand in marriage, and restrained themselves only out of fear of Pablo, whose valor was well known and whose desperation made him capable of madness, it became urgent to take steps to rid the town of that pernicious character.

"Soon, an opportunity to fulfill that wish presented itself to Carmen's relatives. Civil war had broken out, and the government had requested that each of the districts of this State send a certain number of recruits to form new battalions. The prefects in turn made the request of their towns, and since this one is small, with honest, hardworking people, the authorities asked the mayor to send just those who were lazy and dissolute. You are already familiar with the custom of military service as punishment, and condemning those whose are lost to that fate. It is a disgrace."

"And a great one," I responded. "This custom is injurious, and I hope this war will end as soon as possible so that legislators may select a method for forming our army more in keeping with our dignity and our republican system."

"Well then," the priest continued, "on the night before Christmas Eve, an officer presented himself here with his troops, with the intention of taking away his recruits. The town was in an uproar, fearing that they had come to decimate families; the young men hid, and the women cried. But the mayor calmed every down by saying that the prefect had given him permission to hand over just the dissolute, and in the whole place there was only one, Pablo, who would be condemned to military service. And right away the mayor sent for him to be apprehended and brought to the officer.

"When I learned of it, I was sorry to hear of the mayor's decision, but it was no longer possible to change it, and furthermore, Pablo's apprehension was the lightning rod that saved the town's other young men.

"Some pitied the poor boy; but no one dared to plead for his liberty, and the officer took him prisoner.

"It appears that on that evening of the twenty-third, evading the vigilance of his guards, and thanks to his knowledge of the place and his highlander's agility, Pablo was able to escape his prison, which was the town hall, where the troops were quartered, and run to Carmen's house; he called out to her and her mother, who, frightened, answered the door to see what he wanted. Pablo said to the young woman that, just as he had come to speak to her, he could easily escape into the mountains; but he wanted to know, in this moment of utmost seriousness for him, whether he could harbor any hope at all for his feelings to be reciprocated, because if not, he would resign himself to his fate, and go seek out death in the war; but if Carmen felt any affection for him at all, she should tell him, and he would escape right away, work to change his behavior, and make himself worthy of her.

"Carmen considered this for a moment, spoke with her mother, and responded, though with regret, to the young man, that she could not deceive him; that he ought not to have any hope of reciprocation; that her relatives abhorred him, and she would not want to give them trouble by keeping him back, particularly when she had no faith in his promises of reform, because it was already too late for that. And so she was sorry about his fate, but it was not in her power to prevent it.

"Hearing this, Pablo was dejected; he bade farewell to Carmen, and walked slowly back to his prison."

"Ay! That is how it went," said Carmen, sobbing. "It is all my fault . . . everything he has suffered."

"But my daughter," her mother replied. "He was so bad then . . ."

"The next day," the priest continued, "at eight in the morning, the officer left with his troops, who drummed out a march and brought among their ranks the poor boy, tied up, who bowed his head in sorrow when he saw people had come out to stare at him."

"'Goodbye, Pablo!' the women and children repeated, peeking out from behind the doors of their cottages; but he did not hear that beloved voice or see the face of Carmen among the curious.

"That evening of the twenty-fourth, we had our Christmas Eve event, and supper was set out in this very place; but having begun in happiness, the event ended sadly, because when time came for joy, dancing, and commotion, everyone missed that joyous young man who, though dissolute, was, in his lightheartedness, the soul of the town's celebrations.

"'Ay, poor Pablo! Where might he be now?' someone asked.

"'Where he ought to be!' someone else responded. 'In the jail of some nearby town; or kept awake by the cold and tied tightly up in the mountain the troops are crossing.'

"Scarcely had Carmen heard these words when, unable to take anymore, she burst into tears. She had been holding in a great sadness, and she could longer keep her composure. This came as a surprise, because it was common knowledge that she had not loved Pablo. Her sobs made everyone think that though the girl had shown aversion to his disarray, deep down she did love him a little.

"The good mayor grew irritated, as did Carmen's mother, and they withdrew, immediately ending supper in that sad way.

"Three years have passed. We had gotten no news of Pablo until five months ago, when he returned to town; he presented himself to the mayor with his passport and discharge papers, and asked permission to live and work in a part of the mountain six leagues from here. In those two years, there had been a great change in Pablo's character and even his appearance. He had served as a soldier, distinguishing himself among his colleagues for his bravery, his honesty, and his military training, such that he had even been made an officer in that short period of time. But having received many wounds in his campaigns, wounds from which he still suffers, he asked to be discharged so he could rest from the work of war, and his commanders granted his discharge with many commendations.

"Pablo spent only a couple hours in town, changing his military uniform for the garb of a highland laborer, buying some provisions and farm tools, and leaving for his mountain without seeing anyone, Carmen and myself included. Having withdrawn to that place, he began to live like Robinson Crusoe. He chose the wildest part of the mountains, built a hut, tilled the land, and, on excursions to nearby villages, gathered seeds and everything else he needed for his projects.

"His journeys as a soldier through the center of the Republic have served him well. He has acquired ideas about agriculture and horticulture, and has put them into practice here with such success that it is a pleasure to see his little 'patch,' as he humbly calls his land. No, that land is no simple patch, but a beautiful plantation that is quite the achievement. Though the project is still in its infancy, it already shows much promise. His fruit trees are splendid, and his small plantings of corn, wheat, peas, and lentils have started producing a regular harvest. Thanks to him, we have been able to enjoy strawberries as delicious as the best crops from the central part of the country, as he cultivates them in abundance, and he seems to be fond of flowers, as he has planted violets all around, violets like the ones in Mexico City (not scentless like the ones from here), and periwinkle, wild roses, and hollyhock, in addition to all of the rare and aromatic flowers of our mountains. He has planted a small vineyard, and it is him I have charged with caring for my mulberry saplings, which were planted in an area with more suitable temperatures. In sum, he is indefatigable in his labors; he seems possessed by a fever for work. One could say that he wishes to show the town that tossed him from its bosom for his behavior that he did not deserve that ignominy, that it had always been in his power to return to a righteous path, if the person to whom he had made the promise had believed in his words.

"The shepherds of the numerous flocks that graze nearby, as I have told you, adore him, because no sooner is the presence of a wild beast detected in this or that place through the damage wrought, than Pablo volunteers to hunt it down, and he does not rest until he has brought its carcass to the pen at the center of the injured herd. And Pablo will not accept the reward that it is customary to give to hunters of harmful beasts; instead, after bringing the dead tiger, wolf, or leopard, or giving notice of where the beast has been left, he withdraws without another word. The singularity of his character, together with his rare generosity and his fearless bravery, have earned him everyone's affection; but no one can express it the way they would like to, because Pablo shuns the company of people, spending his days in somber taciturnity; and despite the fact that he still suffers greatly from his wounds, he will not turn to anyone for healing, limiting himself to trading a few provisions for the fruits of his fields with highland laborers or villagers passing through. Near his field is his little cabin surrounded by rocks that he has covered in moss and flowers: there he lives like a hermit or a savage, working during the day, and occasionally reading a few books at night, gripped always by a tenacious sadness.

"Moved as I am by his situation, I have gone to see him a few times. He waits for me, gives me gifts, and listens to me, but always resists coming to town. One day at the beginning of winter, when I knew him to be bedridden, suffering because of his wounds, I wished to bring Carmen's mother with me to serve as solace; but as soon as he espied us from afar, he fled to the most harsh and hidden part of the mountain, and we could do nothing but leave him some medicine and provisions, leaving full of regret for not having seen him."

I interrupted: "But that boy is going to end up going crazy, living like that, in the way of Amadís; he must be brought away from that place."

"Undoubtedly," the priest answered. "I have had the same thought myself, and to that end I have put measures into place. You will have understood what the only effective measure could be, because it has not escaped my notice that Pablo is still in love with this girl, and his love only grows by the day; it is just that, haughty by nature, and resentful in the depths of his soul for what he has gone through, he cannot think about the object of his affection, without the shadow of his memories immediately reopening the wound and engendering that desperation that has turned into a dangerous melancholy."

"But in short . . . this girl . . ." I asked, with a rudeness mixed with much curiosity. Carmen did not respond; she covered her face with her hands and sobbed.

"Ah! I understand, my good priest," I continued, "I understand. And it was about time, because the luck of that unhappy lover had begun to oppress me so . . ."

"As you will also grant me," the priest replied, "I could do nothing else—even knowing the true source of Pablo's sorrow—but bide my time, because for nothing in this world would I have wanted to talk to Carmen about the young man's anguish; I feared being the reason that this good and sensible girl would resolve to make a sacrifice of *compassion* for Pablo, or that she would come to feel for him a bit of affection rooted in that same *compassion*. You, captain, being a man of the world, can no doubt immediately comprehend the worth of a *love of compassion*. There is nothing more fragile than that, and no greater misfortune for loving hearts.

"I wanted to know if Carmen had loved Pablo previously, despite his short-comings, and had hidden it from even herself out of modesty and respect for the opinions of her relatives. If that were not the case, I wanted her to at least love him today, convinced of his virtues and holding in esteem his noble character, which is a little fierce, it is true, but always dignified and passionate.

"If I could not know this, any arrangements I might be able to make for my protégé seemed dangerous; and not even to him did I breathe a word, just as he never let me know, not even with a hint, the true reason for his suffering and solitude.

"I did well to wait: love, true love, the kind that bursts forth no matter what hindrances arise, soon came to my aid.

"One day, just three days ago, the good mayor came to see me at my house, called me aside, and told me:

'Brother priest, my family and I are in need of your kindness, because there is a serious matter in which the life of a person we love very much may be at stake.'

'What could it be, my good mayor?' I asked him, taken aback.

'It seems, brother priest, that poor Carmen, my niece, is in love, very much in love, and she can no longer disguise it or have any peace: she is sick, she has no appetite, she cannot sleep, she does not even want to speak.'

'Could it be?' I asked him with alarm, because I feared hearing a revelation that would be entirely contrary to my hopes. 'And who is Carmen in love with, may I know?'

'Yes, señor, you may, and that is precisely why I have come. As you already know, when Pablo, the soldier, was wooing her a few years ago, my sister and I, who felt no affection for the boy because he was messy and a loafer, tried none-theless to learn if she had feelings for him, and were satisfied that she did not, and loathed him as we did. That is why I decided to hand him over to the troops; thus we could rid the town of a noxious type and free my niece of his impertinence. But you will recall that that same Christmas Eve, as we were talking about Pablo at my house during dinner, Carmen began to cry. Well then: after that, her mother started observing her closely; and even though she continued to notice nothing amiss, she became convinced that her daughter loved the young man. And she was convinced because Carmen would not hear anything of marriage, wanting nothing to do with the proposals made by several of the town's honorable, well-to-do young men. When there was talk of Pablo, Carmen would lose her color, grow sad, and retire to her room; in short, we never spoke of him again, but it seems that she never forgot him.

'In this way, the years passed; but since Pablo's return, my niece has lost her composure entirely: the day we learned he was here, we all noticed her turmoil, though we could not tell whether it was from joy, fear, or surprise. Later, once she found out what kind of life Pablo leads in the mountains, she would sigh, and sometimes cry, until at last my sister decided to ask her frankly what was wrong and whether she loved the young man. Carmen responded that she does, and always has, and that is the reason she is sad; but she believes Pablo must despise her now, as he must consider her to be the cause of all his suffering, and that must explain his not wanting to come to town or see her. She said she would like to speak to him, to ask his forgiveness if she has offended him, and to remove this thorn from her heart, as contentment will elude her for as long as his grudge lives. This is what has been happening, brother; and now I come to beg you to go see Pablo and ask him to come, with the pretext of the supper taking place the day after tomorrow, so Carmen can talk to him, and seek redress, if possible, and find out whether the boy still loves her; I am afraid my niece may fall ill otherwise.'

"Captain, you will have already guessed my joy: not even if I had arranged it myself could it have turned out better. I capitalized on a trip away from town for a confession to hurry into the mountain, saw Pablo, urged him to come, and he agreed . . . I find it very strange that he has not kept his promise."

As the priest finished saying this, a shepherd crossed the patio and came to tell the priest and the mayor that Pablo was resting at the gate, for he was extremely sick and had made the journey little by little, and had arrived very tired.

A shout of joy rang through town: the mayor and the priest got up to go see the young man; Carmen's mother looked quite uneasy, and Carmen started to tremble, her face going deathly pale . . . "Let us go, my girl," I told her. "Be calm; the only way he could not die of love before you is if his heart is made of stone."

Carmen shook her head uncertainly, and in that instant, the mayor and the priest entered, a young man propped up between them—tall, dark, with a dark beard and dark hair that emphasized his great pallor, and in whose sad gaze one could see the firmness of a proud character.

It was Pablo.

He was dressed like a highlander and was carrying a long, gnarled walking stick.

"Viva Pablo!" shouted the young people, tossing their hats into the air; the women wept, the men came to greet him. The mayor steered him toward his sister and niece, saying:

"Come here, you rogue, this is where you are needed—if you have a good heart, you must forgive us all."

When Pablo saw Carmen, he seemed to waver with emotion, growing paler; but then, drawing himself up, he said, in an agitated way:

"Forgive, señor! What do I have to forgive? To the contrary, I am the one who ought to ask for forgiveness for how much I offended this town . . . !"

Then Carmen stood up, flushed and tremulous, and walked toward the young man; lowering her gaze, she said:

"Yes, Pablo, we ask for your forgiveness; I ask for your forgiveness for the events of three years ago . . . I am the cause of your suffering . . . and for that, God well knows I have wept. I beg you not to resent me."

The young woman could not go on, and had to sit down to hide her emotion and her tears.

Pablo was astonished. It was evident that something extraordinary was happening in his soul, as he was twisting from side to side to make sure he was not dreaming. But a moment later, hearing Carmen's mother, with her hands clasped in a pleading way, say, "Pablo, forgive her!" he let two plump tears slip from his eyes, and made an effort to speak.

"But, señora," he replied. "But, Carmen, who told you that I resented you? Why would I resent you? I was dissolute, good mayor, and that is why you handed me over to the troops. A deed well done: that was how I corrected myself and became an upstanding man. I was a loafer, a lost boy, Carmen: you were a good and virtuous girl, and that is why when I spoke to you of love, you told me you felt no affection for me. Very well done: In what way was it your duty to love me? You did more than enough, in not feeling shame to hear my words. I am the one who must ask you for forgiveness, for having been insolent with you, for having impeded, perhaps, your ability to love as your heart prescribed. When I think about this, I feel sorrow."

"Oh! No, no, Pablo," the young woman hastened to say. "Please do not let that upset you, because there was no one I loved then . . . or at any point after," she added, embarrassed. "And if you do not believe me, ask around in town . . . I swear, there has been no one I have loved . . ."

"Except you, my friend," I dared say to Pablo, impatient to draw together those two lovelorn hearts. "Come now," I added. "The resolution of this matter requires a bit of military character. You who have been a military man, lend me a hand. I know everything; I know you adore this girl, and in doing so you prove that you are worth much. She loves you too, and if you doubt it, let those tears tell you so, and the suffering she has felt since you left to serve the Homeland. May you two be happy, by Jove!" It was time; they were both dying for not wanting to confess their feelings. "Pablo, come to your love, and tell her you are the happiest man on earth; unclasp those hands, lovely Carmen, and let this boy read in your beautiful eyes all the love you feel for him; and may the judge and the priest waste no time in bringing this matter to a conclusion."

The two lovers stretched out their hands, smiling, and I received an ovation for my little exhortations and frank way of arranging matrimony. The shepherds sang and played the most joyful sonatas on their guitars, pipes, and tambourines; the children set off fireworks; and the chimes that announce dawn's arrival on Christmas, inviting the faithful to come pray in the first hours of the great Christian day, were a timely addition to the boisterous concert.

When the deep peals of the bell began to sound, slow and rhythmic, signaling that it was time for prayer, all noise ceased; all those hearts overflowing with joy and tenderness lifted themselves to God with a unanimous vow of gratitude, for the blessings he had deigned to bestow upon that innocent and humble town.

Everyone prayed in silence: the priest preferred it thus so as to align more closely with the spirit of sincerity that should characterize true worship, and he let each person address their prayer to the heavens as their faith and their feelings prescribed.

And so everyone—the elderly, the young men, the children, and the women— prayed in seclusion. The priest seemed absorbed and was shedding tears, and all shadow of melancholy had disappeared from his sweet and honorable countenance, which was lit up with an ineffable bliss. The town's schoolteacher had knelt down beside his wife and children, who embraced him with affection, remembering the danger he had been in three years before; the mayor, like a biblical patriarch, put his hands on the heads of his children, who were gathered around him; uncle Francisco and aunt Juana too, between their children, murmured their prayers and wept; Gertrudis held her beautiful daughter, who had bowed her head as if overwhelmed with happiness, and Pablo sobbed, perhaps for the first time, still holding between his the delicate white hand of his adored Carmen, who had just flung open his doors to paradise. I myself had forgotten all my sorrows, feeling happy as I contemplated that portrait of simple virtue and a true and modest bliss, which I had searched for in vain in opulent cities and a society stirred by terrible passions.

When the daybreak prayers had concluded, the gathering did as well, and we bade farewell to the dignified mayor and the future spouses, who stayed behind with him to finish their vigil, as did many other neighbors; and we went to rest, walking with a quick step, because at that hour, as was often the case in winter at those altitudes, the snow was starting to come down thick, and the flakes were starting to bend the branches of the trees, cover the cabins' straw roofs, and carpet the ground all around.

I stayed one more day in the town and left on the twenty-sixth, but not without embracing tight to my chest that most virtuous of priests whom I had been so fortunate to encounter, and whose friendship has been of great value to me since.

Never—and you will have already understood this from my story—have I been able to forget "that beautiful Christmas spent in the mountains."

1871

IGNACIO MANUEL ALTAMIRANO (1834–1893) was a writer, journalist, and politician. Born into an indigenous Chontal family, he founded several publications, including the review *El Renacimiento* (The Renaissance) and the newspaper *El Correo de México* (The Mexico Post) and was the author of three novels. He supported liberal causes during the Reform War and the Second Franco-Mexican War, and after serving as consul in Spain and France, Altamirano died in San Remo, Italy.

CARMEN BOULLOSA (1954–) is one of Mexico's leading novelists, poets, and playwrights. Born in Mexico City, the author of eighteen novels and fifteen poetry collections has been honored with Guggenheim and Cullman Center Fellowships as well as the Xavier Villaurrutia Award. Currently, Boullosa is a Distinguished Lecturer at City College of New York. Her novels in English include *Texas: The Great Theft*, *The Book of Anna*, and the forthcoming *The Book of Eve*, all translated by Samantha Schnee.

SANDRA CISNEROS (1954–) is an American writer best known for her 1983 novel *The House on Mango Street*. An icon of Chicana literature, she was born and raised in Chicago as the only daughter in a family of seven. The recipient of two National Endowment for the Arts Fellowships and a MacArthur Fellowship, she founded the Macondo Writers Workshop, an association of socially engaged writers, in 1995. Her books have been translated into twenty-five languages. She has lived in San Miguel de Allende since 2013.

SOR JUANA INÉS DE LA CRUZ (1648–1695) was a poet, dramatist, composer, scholar, and Hieronymite nun who lived and wrote in Mexico during Spanish colonial rule. Known as "The Tenth Muse" and "The Phoenix of America," she was born in San Miguel Nepantla and joined a convent in Mexico City at the age of nineteen. She went on to author, among other works, the long poem *First Dream* and the "Reply to Sor Filotea," a letter written in defense of women's right to secular and religious scholarship.

AMPARO DÁVILA (1928–2020), the author of several story collections, has in recent years been recognized as one of Mexico's finest renderers of the uncanny. Born in the town of Pinos in Zacatecas, she published her first collection in 1950, moved to Mexico City in 1954, and went on to receive the Xavier Villaurrutia Award and the Medalla Bellas Artes. Her first book in English, *The Houseguest and Other Stories*, was published in 2018 in a translation by Audrey Harris and Matthew Gleeson.

LAURA ESQUIVEL (1950–) is a writer best known for her 1989 novel *Like Water for Chocolate*, the film adaptation of which went on to become one of the highest-grossing foreign films ever released in the United States. Born and based in Mexico City, she began writing while teaching kindergarten in the 1970s. *Like Water for Chocolate*, her first novel, has been translated into thirty languages. Between 2012 and 2018, she served as a federal representative in the Mexican Chamber of Deputies.

CARLOS FUENTES (1928–2012) was one of the principal voices of the "Boom," the period in 1960s and 1970s when Latin American writers such as Gabriel García Márquez and Julio Cortázar came to global prominence. Born in Panama City into a Mexican diplomatic family, Fuentes published his first novel *Where the Air Is Clear* in 1958 to immediate acclaim. He received many honors, including the Xavier Villaurrutia Award, the Rómulo Gallegos Prize, the Miguel de Cervantes Prize, and the Belisario Domínguez Medal of Honor.

CARLOS MONSIVÁIS (1938–2010) was a writer, journalist, and cultural critic who for several decades was one of Mexico's most widely recognizable chroniclers of contemporary life. Born in Mexico City, he became known for his commentary on the political and social issues of his time. His longest-running column, titled "*Por mi madre, bohemios*" (For My Mother, Bohemians) was published almost uninterrupted in a number of newspapers between 1972 and 2010.

FABIO MORÁBITO (1955–) is a writer and translator. Born in Egypt to Italian parents, he moved at the age of fourteen to Mexico City and has lived there ever since. He is the author of four volumes of poetry, four story collections, two books of essays, a children's book, and two novels—one of which was awarded the Xavier Villaurrutia Award—as well as the translator into Spanish of a number of twentieth-century Italian poets.

AMADO NERVO (1870–1919) was a writer, journalist, and diplomat. He was born in Tepic in the state of Nayarit, in 1894. After a stint as a journalist in the Sinaloan city of Mazatlán, he moved to Mexico City, where he became one of the leading figures of Modernist poetry. A contemporary of Luis Gonzaga Urbina at *Revista azul* (Blue Review), he also cofounded the influential journal *Revista moderna* (Modern Review). He died in Montevideo, Uruguay, while serving as Mexico's ambassador.

LUIS GONZAGA URBINA (1864–1934) was a poet and journalist. Born in Mexico City, he published his first poems at the age of seventeen and, like Amado Nervo, was known for his contributions to Modernist poetry. He was the author of well over a dozen volumes of chronicles, scholarship, and poetry. In 1913, he was named director of the National Library of Mexico, but he left that post in 1915, when the Mexican Revolution sent him into self-exile first in Havana and then in Madrid, where he died.

"*Birth of Christ, with Comment on the Bee*"
"*Christmas Night*"
translated by Timothy Adès

Excerpt from *Like Water for Chocolate*
translated by Carol Christensen and Thomas Christensen

"*The Discomfiting Brother*"
translated by Edith Grossman

"*Moses and Gaspar*"
translated by Audrey Harris and Matthew Gleeson

"*The Double Cat Syndrome*"
translated by Jennifer Staff Johnson

"*The Toppled Tree*"
translated by Andrea G. Labinger

Excerpt from *Christmas in the Mountains*
"*Carmen and Pablo*" from *Christmas in the Mountains*
"*The Old Man*"
"*The Tragedy of the Toy*"
"*The Two Christmases*"
translated by Jennifer Shyue

A VERY GERMAN CHRISTMAS

This collection brings together traditional and contemporary holiday stories from Austria, Switzerland and Germany. You'll find classic works by the Brothers Grimm, Johann Wolfgang von Goethe, Heinrich Heine, Thomas Mann, Rainer Maria Rilke, Hermann Hesse, Joseph Roth and Arthur Schnitzler, as well as more recent tales by writers like Heinrich Böll, Peter Stamm and Martin Suter.

A VERY SCANDINAVIAN CHRISTMAS

The best Scandinavian holiday stories including classics by Hans Christian Andersen, Nobel Prize winner Selma Lagerlöf, August Strindberg as well as popular Norwegian author Karl Ove Knausgaard. These Nordic tales—coming from the very region where much traditional Christmas imagery originates—convey a festive spirit laden with lingonberries, elks, gnomes and aquavit in abundance. A smorgasbord of unexpected literary gifts sure to provide plenty of pleasure and *hygge*, that specifically Scandinavian blend of coziness and contentment.

A VERY FRENCH CHRISTMAS

A continuation of the very popular Very Christmas Series, this collection brings together the best French Christmas stories of all time in an elegant and vibrant collection featuring classics by Guy de Maupassant and Alphonse Daudet, plus stories by the esteemed twentieth century author Irène Némirovsky and contemporary writers Dominique Fabre and Jean-Philippe Blondel. With a holiday spirit conveyed through sparkling Paris streets, opulent feasts, wandering orphans, flickering desire, and more than a little wine, this collection proves that the French have mastered Christmas.

A VERY ITALIAN CHRISTMAS

This volume brings together the best Italian Christmas stories of all time in a fascinating collection featuring classic tales and contemporary works. With writing that dates from the Renaissance to the present day, from Boccaccio to Pirandello, as well as Anna Maria Ortese, Natalia Ginzburg and Nobel laureate Grazia Deledda, this choice selection delights and intrigues. Like everything the Italians do, this is Christmas with its very own verve and flair, the perfect literary complement to a *Buon Natale italiano*.

A VERY RUSSIAN CHRISTMAS

This is Russian Christmas celebrated in supreme pleasure and pain by the greatest of writers, from Dostoevsky and Tolstoy to Chekhov and Teffi. The dozen stories in this collection will satisfy every reader, and with their wit, humor, and tenderness, packed full of sentimental songs, footmen, whirling winds, solitary nights, snow drifts, and hopeful children, the collection proves that Nobody Does Christmas Like the Russians.

A VERY IRISH CHRISTMAS

This collection transports readers to the Emerald Isle with stories and poems sure to bring holiday cheer. The anthology is packed with beloved classics, forgotten treasures, and modern masterpieces. You'll find wondrous works by James Joyce, Elizabeth Bowen, W. B. Yeats, Anne Enright, William Trevor, Colm Tóibín, Bernard MacLaverty and many more.

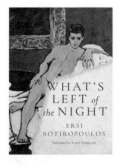

WHAT'S LEFT OF THE NIGHT by Ersi Sotiropoulos

Constantine Cavafy arrives in Paris in 1897 on a trip that will deeply shape his future and push him toward his poetic inclination. With this lyrical novel, tinged with an hallucinatory eroticism that unfolds over three unforgettable days, celebrated Greek author Ersi Sotiropoulos depicts Cavafy in the midst of a journey of self-discovery across a continent on the brink of massive change. A stunning portrait of a budding author—before he became C.P. Cavafy, one of the 20th century's greatest poets—that illuminates the complex relationship of art, life, and the erotic desires that trigger creativity.

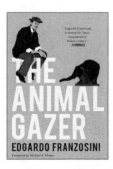

THE ANIMAL GAZER by Edgardo Franzosini

A hypnotic novel inspired by the strange and fascinating life of sculptor Rembrandt Bugatti, brother of the fabled automaker. Bugatti obsessively observes and sculpts the baboons, giraffes, and panthers in European zoos, finding empathy with their plight and identifying with their life in captivity. Rembrandt Bugatti's work, now being rediscovered, is displayed in major art museums around the world and routinely fetches large sums at auction. Edgardo Franzosini recreates the young artist's life with intense lyricism, passion, and sensitivity.

ALLMEN AND THE DRAGONFLIES by Martin Suter

Johann Friedrich von Allmen has exhausted his family fortune by living in Old World grandeur despite present-day financial constraints. Forced to downscale, Allmen inhabits the garden house of his former Zurich estate, attended by his Guatemalan butler, Carlos. This is the first of a series of humorous, fast-paced detective novels devoted to a memorable gentleman thief. A thrilling art heist escapade infused with European high culture and luxury that doesn't shy away from the darker side of human nature.

THE MADELEINE PROJECT by Clara Beaudoux

A young woman moves into a Paris apartment and discovers a storage room filled with the belongings of the previous owner, a certain Madeleine who died in her late nineties, and whose treasured possessions nobody seems to want. In an audacious act of journalism driven by personal curiosity and humane tenderness, Clara Beaudoux embarks on *The Madeleine Project*, documenting what she finds on Twitter with text and photographs, introducing the world to an unsung 20th century figure.

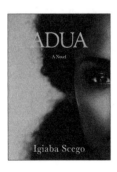

ADUA by Igiaba Scego

Adua, an immigrant from Somalia to Italy, has lived in Rome for nearly forty years. She came seeking freedom from a strict father and an oppressive regime, but her dreams of film stardom ended in shame. Now that the civil war in Somalia is over, her homeland calls her. She must decide whether to return and reclaim her inheritance, but also how to take charge of her own story and build a future.

IF VENICE DIES by Salvatore Settis

Internationally renowned art historian Salvatore Settis ignites a new debate about the Pearl of the Adriatic and cultural patrimony at large. In this fiery blend of history and cultural analysis, Settis argues that "hit-and-run" visitors are turning Venice and other landmark urban settings into shopping malls and theme parks. This is a passionate plea to secure the soul of Venice, written with consummate authority, wide-ranging erudition and élan.

THE MADONNA OF NOTRE DAME by Alexis Ragougneau

Fifty thousand people jam into Notre Dame Cathedral to celebrate the Feast of the Assumption. The next morning, a beautiful young woman clothed in white kneels at prayer in a cathedral side chapel. But when someone accidentally bumps against her, her body collapses. She has been murdered. This thrilling novel illuminates shadowy corners of the world's most famous cathedral, shedding light on good and evil with suspense, compassion and wry humor.

THE YEAR OF THE COMET by Sergei Lebedev

A story of a Russian boyhood and coming of age as the Soviet Union is on the brink of collapse. Lebedev depicts a vast empire coming apart at the seams, transforming a very public moment into something tender and personal, and writes with stunning beauty and shattering insight about childhood and the growing consciousness of a boy in the world.

THE LAST WEYNFELDT by Martin Suter

Adrian Weynfeldt is an art expert in an international auction house, a bachelor in his mid-fifties living in a grand Zurich apartment filled with costly paintings and antiques. Always correct and well-mannered, he's given up on love until one night—entirely out of character for him—Weynfeldt decides to take home a ravishing but unaccountable young woman and gets embroiled in an art forgery scheme that threatens his buttoned up existence. This refined page-turner moves behind elegant bourgeois facades into darker recesses of the heart.

THE LAST SUPPER by Klaus Wivel

Alarmed by the oppression of 7.5 million Christians in the Middle East, journalist Klaus Wivel traveled to Iraq, Lebanon, Egypt, and the Palestinian territories to learn about their fate. He found a minority under threat of death and humiliation, desperate in the face of rising Islamic extremism and without hope their situation will improve. An unsettling account of a severely beleaguered religious group living, so it seems, on borrowed time. Wivel asks, Why have we not done more to protect these people?

New Vessel Press

To purchase these titles and for more information please visit newvesselpress.com.